EUROPE
ASIA
SHANGHAI, CHINA
JAPAN
S. CHINA SEA
PACIFIC OCEAN
INDIAN OCEAN
JAVA
AUSTRALIA

'Round the World

Takashi Sails Home

For Hanna
Smooth Sailing
and
Adventure in your life.
Lucinda
7.14.11

'ROUND THE WORLD

TAKASHI SAILS HOME

LUCINDA HATHAWAY

ILLUSTRATED BY
MARILYN GANSS

DOWN THE SHORE
PUBLISHING
WEST CREEK, NEW JERSEY

Box 100, West Creek, NJ 08092
www.down-the-shore.com

Printed in China.
10 9 8 7 6 5 4 3 2 1
First printing, 2008.

Book design by Leslee Ganss

Library of Congress Cataloging-in-Publication Data

Hathaway, Lucinda Churchman.
'Round the world : Takashi sails home / Lucinda Hathaway.
p. cm.
Summary: In 1901, Takashi, who was shanghaied from Japan and brought to the United States, meets the captain of a Maine schooner and his son and soon finds himself a cabin boy on the newly-commissioned ship Astral, which is sailing for the Far East.
ISBN 978-1-59322-034-1
[1. Adventure and adventurers--Fiction. 2. Japanese--New England--Fiction. 3. Seafaring life--Fiction. 4. New England--History--20th century--Fiction.] I. Title. II. Title: Around the world.
PZ7.H2835Rou 2008
[Fic]--dc22

2008004719

In memory of my friend Helen Cross,
and our many happy days sailing
in Great Egg Harbor Bay.

Contents

Fact and Fiction

WRITING HISTORICAL FICTION means that the writer has found a piece of interesting history — fact — and has woven a story — fiction — around the history. The story must not contradict the historical setting. For example, it would not be appropriate for Tashi and Clarabel to learn how to use a computer program or read a radar screen because neither of those devices was available to sailing ships in 1902. It is also a fact that in 1901 the word "ship" would have only been used to describe a sailing vessel with three or more masts, all rigged with square sails. At that time the generic term for watercrafts/boats would have been vessel. Today we refer to large watercrafts of all types as ships, and small crafts as boats. Keep that in mind as you read the story.

For me this journey started with the fact that the *Sindia* wrecked in Ocean City, N.J., on December 15, 1901. In the Ocean City Historical Museum hangs a half model with the label, "Carved by the Japanese Cabin Boy." That was the beginning, and the basis for *Takashi's Voyage: The Wreck of the Sindia,* the first half of this story in which Takashi is stranded in America.

To answer the question, "How does Takashi get home?" I found a bit of history about the bark *Astral,* launched in Bath, Maine at Sewell's Shipyard on December 8, 1900 (fact). For purposes of my story I changed the date to January 11, 1902 (fiction). Another interesting piece of history was that my favorite windjammer, the *Lewis R. French*, built in 1871 in Christmas Cove, Maine, had, at the same time, been a coasting schooner sailing from Maine, delivering cargo to ports along the northeast coast of America. It is also historical fact that coasting schooners brought the granite for the Brooklyn Bridge to New York from Maine as well as Christmas trees and other cargo. *'Round the World: Takashi Sails Home* is based on these facts of history plus stories woven of time-appropriate fiction.

While reading and researching this book I visited many of the places I write about, sailed some of the waters, and tried some of the art forms. Perhaps readers would like to know the effect of time and history on some of these places. Here is some of what I observed:

Kobe, Japan ~ I did not see one sailing vessel at the harbor side of Kobe. The skyline is studded with high-rise buildings and cranes, used to unload the container ships that come to this busy port. At night the lights glimmer and the Ferris wheel at the quayside park turns round and round.

Brooklyn Bridge ~ Walking across the footpath on the bridge is still a thrill. From the center of the bridge one can see the Statue of Liberty and the South Street Seaport Museum at the base of the bridge. The bark, *Peking,* is tied at the wharf, and if you walk aboard you will have an idea of life aboard these huge sailing vessels.

Bath, Maine ~ Today the waterfront is still busy with ships being repaired and built at Bath Iron Works. You can learn more about the *Astral* and other sailing vessels built in Bath at the Maine Maritime Museum, located on the riverfront.

Searsport, Maine ~ It is easy to imagine how this small town must have looked a hundred years ago when you walk along the waterfront. I found a piece of blue and white china in the sand as I walked there, and later it was identified as 19th-century pottery used as ballast on the sailing vessels that used this port. Searsport is still a deepwater port for ocean-going tankers. The Penobscot Maritime Museum, in the middle of town in a collection of historic houses, is a good place to learn more about sailing.

Lewis R. French ~ This coasting schooner is part of the Maine Windjammer fleet that sails from Camden, Maine. My husband and I have sailed on the *French* many times and it is always fun.

Paper cranes ~ Origami is the ancient Japanese art of folding paper. The folded paper crane is a symbol of peace. At Peace Park in Hiroshima, Japan, I saw hundreds of thousands of paper cranes folded by children worldwide symbolizing their hope for peace throughout the world.

Sumi-e ~ I had great fun practicing Japanese brush stroke painting in classes in Florida. The routine and exacting nature of this painting contrasts with its freedom of stroke and individual expression. Beautiful examples of *sumi-e* can be seen in any museum that has an Asian art collection.

Staten Island Ferry ~ From the ferry stop on Staten Island you can walk to Sailor's Snug Harbor, which today is the Snug Harbor Cultural Center. Taking a ride on the ferry will allow you to view the Brooklyn Bridge from the water and see the Statue of Liberty in the distance. Look for the tugboats. It is hard to miss the McAllister tugboats working in New York Harbor, as they have for the last hundred fifty years or more.

Researching the history and learning about a period in time is great fun. One of the most enjoyable research experiences for me was to sail on the American tall ship, *Rose,* from Dartmouth in Southern England to France, across the English Channel. We had glorious weather and the seventeen sails on this full-rigged ship were set as we sailed "full and by" to our destination. It was easy for me to pretend I was Tashi sailing 'round the world. Today the *Rose*, a replica of a 1776 sailing ship, is docked at the San Diego Maritime Museum. Since I sailed on her she has had her own adventure in the movie *Master and Commander* with Russell Crowe, based on the novel by Patrick O'Brian. The *Rose* was transformed into *HMS Surprise* and became a star.

Upon the completion of this book, I will have sailed 'round the world using my imagination and my word processor, in the company of a brave, talented boy — Takashi. Using history as the basis for much of this adventure, the rest grew in my imagination — which travels with me wherever I go.

Wishing each of you smooth sailing, and a lifetime of adventure,

Lucinda Hathaway
Longboat Key, Florida

Chapter 1

New York City

"COOKIE, THAT HURTS!" BLOOD TRICKLED down Takashi's neck as the old sailor, Cookie, forced the gold ring through his earlobe. They were standing by Pier #16 on Front Street, New York Harbor, in the shadow of the Brooklyn Bridge.

"You're a Cape Horner and I want you to have my earring." Cookie grabbed a handful of snow and washed away the blood. Done! Takashi had a gold earring in a sore left ear marking him a sailor who had sailed around Cape Horn. He pulled his wool cap down over his throbbing ear and watched Cookie sling a duffle bag over his shoulder and prepare to leave.

"*Domo arigato,*" the Japanese boy said. "Thank you."

"You're welcome, lad," said Cookie. "Wish ye'd come along. I could find you a bunk in Liverpool and ye'd find passage to Japan there." Cookie almost hugged the boy but the old sailor was too tough to do it.

"I must find ship here in New York and go home." Takashi's voice sounded firm, but he was not sure he was making the right decision.

Takashi and the entire crew had been rescued by the lifesavers six days earlier when their vessel, the *Sindia,* wrecked 300 feet off the boardwalk in Ocean City, New Jersey. The huge bark was stuck on a sandbar very close to shore. Drying out and getting warm took three days. The officers and crew rode the train to Philadelphia where the British Admiralty tried and convicted their Captain MacKenzie and first officer, George Stewart. The penalties were harsh. Captain MacKenzie lost his captain's papers and George Stewart lost his rank. The officers were found to be responsible for running a ship aground in charted waters, an offense of negligence.

Philadelphia can be a cold, dark city in December. During the court trial the entire crew was cramped in the Seaman's Institute lodgings, miserable damp cold rooms. There they waited, hoping their captain would not be charged with negligence. The crew felt that the wreck was an accident. Once the guilty verdict announced, they sadly left their captain and headed to the grand port of New York where the seamen hoped to find ships to sail them home to England. Liverpool, England, was the homeport for most of the *Sindia* sailors.

Takashi was determined to find a ship sailing to Japan or Shanghai. He was certain that if he could get as far as Shanghai, going home to Japan would be possible. Every day ships from Shanghai called at his uncle's warehouse in Kobe, Japan. Takashi would find a way home.

Today he watched Cookie, Charlie, John Hand and the other crew of the *Sindia* board the *Georgian,* bound for Liverpool. The *Admiral Dewey,* a small red tugboat, strained to pull the huge sailing ship away from her

berth. Back and forth the tug captain edged his vessel from one side to the other pushing the *Georgian* into the East River. Takashi's friends waved from the deck. The *Georgian* would sail to Liverpool in eleven days.

Takashi, alone in the big city of New York, longed for his home halfway round the world. Determination, pluck and having survived the trip from Japan made him know in his heart he could return. His older brother, Sami, would be waiting for him — that he knew. Aunt Lei and Uncle Hiroshi would be wondering what had happened to Takashi. Uncle Hiroshi treated his nephews as live-in students and gave them little affection. He forced them to study history and geography. Learn, learn, learn was his mantra. Takashi and Sami respected their uncle but loved Aunt Lei, who treated them as the sons she did not have. Somewhere in the balance of discipline and devotion was a home that Takashi missed and wanted to see again.

He walked down Front Street counting the sailing vessels lining the waterfront. Bowsprits encroached on the street. The figureheads provided a fanciful display of mermaids and monsters all staring down at the young boy walking along the quayside. The jumble of masts and rigging along the waterfront made a puzzle of a proportion that only a sailor could understand. Takashi walked all the way to the end of the island of Manhattan, where he could see the *Georgian's* masts getting smaller and smaller as she headed down the river and out to sea.

It was a pearl grey December day in New York City. A group of sailors were gathered in the park across the street from the big round Custom House. One of the sailors pointed at Takashi and the rest turned to stare.

"There's one of those sailors from Asia. Those slanty eyed foreigners are taking away our jobs," the angry man shouted.

"He's just a boy. Leave him alone," said another sailor.

"Go back where you came from," shouted the first sailor, waving his fist.

Takashi pulled the collar of his pea coat up around his neck. He pulled his hat down around his ears and walked quickly toward a policeman twirling his stick, protection if needed. Takashi was sure the men were angry because they did not get berths on sailing vessels. All kinds of foreign sailors were in port and often captains would choose to take foreign sailors on one-way excursions. If they hired American sailors they would have to take them back to America. Captains wanted to make money and were not interested in paying or feeding sailors one more day than was necessary. The American sailors wanted jobs.

Takashi was alone and scared. He could go back to the New York Seaman's Institute and stay the night. Cookie had taken him to this place run by Christian brothers. In every major port in the whole world sailors could always find a dry bed at a Seaman's Institute. These boarding houses welcomed sailors who were far from home. In his pocket a little American money jingled, his wages for the long trip from Japan to New Jersey. He had stowed his duffle with his prized half-model of the *Sindia* at the Institute. Brother Mark, the man in charge of the rooms, expected him to come back for the night. All day he had to stay out of trouble and find something to eat. As he walked back up Front Street in the cold dark, he kept his head down and hoped that other sailors would not notice that he was a foreigner. New York was not kind to a small boy with no home or friends.

Takashi smelled food cooking. There was a cart with a charcoal burner cooking sausages.

"How much, one sausage?" he asked.

"That will be a nickel," replied the cook waving his fork over his head with a hand clad in green knitted gloves with the fingers cut off so he could cook.

Takashi fished in his pocket and pulled out a shiny coin and handed it to the man. In turn he was handed a sausage in a roll wrapped in waxed paper.

"Try a little mustard on that," said the cook and dabbed some yellow sauce on the sausage. "Here's a cup of coffee to go with it and I put lots of sugar and milk in it." He gave the boy a mug full of brown, steaming liquid.

Takashi tasted the sausage with its bitey yellow sauce and greedily drank the coffee. He thought of the nice tea that Aunt Lei brewed in her beautiful painted pots and how delicately she poured it into thin porcelain cups. Aunt Lei would not like to eat sausages cooked by a stranger on a busy street corner. Takashi enjoyed every bite of the food, yet longed for tea and his Aunt's good cooking.

Darkness and quiet fell over the waterfront. A quiet moment after a busy day wrapped Takashi in its grip. All of the restaurants and bars along the riverfront were filled with sailors and longshoremen drinking their last drinks before heading home for the night. Takashi could hear the loud voices and the music drifting out into the deserted street where he walked. Overhead, the Brooklyn Bridge bustled with people walking home from work. Takashi could see the walkers on the upper level of the bridge and thought that he would like to do that some morning, not at night when he had no idea where to go on the other side.

It was time to head back to the Seaman's Institute, not far off the waterfront. He would speak to Brother Mark and see if there were any new sailors who might help him find a berth on a vessel sailing to Japan. As he crossed the cobbled street in front of a noisy bar a man came flying out of the door with another chasing him swinging a bottle in his hand.

"I'm gonna get you! You're a devil and I'm gonna get you," the man screamed.

Takashi ducked into a doorway and watched as several others joined in the fight on the street. He was scared. The police came to break up the brawl and hauled two of the sailors away in the police wagon. They would sober up in jail. This kind of incident also happened on the waterfront in Kobe where Takashi lived. Because the sailors were so rough, Aunt Lei forbade the boys to go to the waterfront. Takashi and Sami did not listen to her, and because of their disobedience Takashi had been forced to sail on the *Sindia.* One night, he and Sami had watched the sailors load a contraband golden Buddha onto the *Sindia*. When the sailors spotted the boys they chased them. His brother got away. Takashi was caught and carried aboard and forced to sail halfway round the world only to find himself shipwrecked on the beach in Ocean City, New Jersey, on the east coast of America.

Takashi watched the fight. The noise and shouting and punching and crying of the two men was scary. When blood poured down the face of one of the sailors, he could not help but think of his Aunt Lei and know that she was correct about the waterfront. It was a dangerous place.

Takashi hurried on to his bunk at the Institute where he would be safe for the night. It had been a long, sad day. Saying goodbye to the sailors from the *Sindia* and watching them sail off to England was hard. Takashi was alone and scared and glad to see the light over the door of the Seaman's Institute. He would be warm and welcome. But would he be able to find a way to sail home to Japan tomorrow?

Chapter 2

Snug Harbor

AFTER A BREAKFAST OF BACON AND EGGS and coffee, eaten at the Seaman's Institute, Takashi took his duffle and headed down to the wharf. While standing on Pier #17 he saw a curious little sailboat appear. It looked like a tree afloat. With the mainsail atop a mass of fir trees, the boat drifted with the current headed to a pier not far from where Tashi had watched his friends depart yesterday on the *Georgian*.

Takashi could see a boy standing in the floating shrubbery at the bow of the schooner. He was waist deep in greenery. A red-bearded man in yellow oilskins maneuvered the boat to the dock. Takashi waved to the boy and he waved back. Running on South Street and trying to keep the floating bush in sight was not easy. It was a busy Friday and all of the fishmongers were carting their fish to waiting delivery vans. Takashi and the boy maintained their waving signals. When Takashi saw the boat turn to a wharf, he hurried and was waiting alongside.

"Hey there, lend a hand," yelled the boy on the boat, and he threw a line to Takashi, who caught it and looped it over the cleat by his foot on the wharf.

"We have to berth in that space farther down. Do you think you can help me warp her into place?" asked the boy.

In answer, Takashi grabbed the line and walked slowly down the pier pulling the boat overflowing with fir trees behind him as the boy fended off the dock and other obstacles. It was a slow process but the floating ship finally responded to Tashi's tugs and soon she was in the spot assigned. Tashi tied off the bow and the boy hopped onto the wharf with the stern line.

"Thank you," said the boy extending his hand. "You were a big help. My dad and I are on our own. We sure did need you. My name is Joe. What's yours?"

"Tashi," replied the boy.

"Where you from?" asked Joe.

"From Japan. Kobe is my home," said Tashi

"Japan, gee, that's halfway round the world," said Joe.

"Is this your ship?" asked Tashi

"It's not a ship. It's a schooner. Name is *Lewis R. French* and hails from Searsport, Maine. That's where the granite for that bridge is from," he pointed to the Brooklyn Bridge looming over their heads. "My grandpa coasted some of the granite to New York on the *French.* Now we are hauling Christmas trees and lumber. We'll sell the trees today, get Mom and Billy, that's my little brother, a present tomorrow and sail on the tide tomorrow morning. Gotta be home for Christmas or Ma will skin us alive."

"How far away is Maine?" Tashi was puzzled.

"Three day sail."

"Joe, quit your jawing! Get the spring line set and get those trees on shore. I can see the carts waiting to haul them uptown. You, boy! Can you help? I'll pay you."

"That's my dad, Cap'n Pease," explained Joe. "Can you help me? We can get these trees unloaded in no time if we stay with it. What do you say?"

"I can help." Tashi was glad for the talk and the job. When the *Georgian* sailed yesterday Tashi was left alone in this big, foreign city of New York. Now, he had a job and maybe a friend.

Joe handed a tree up to Tashi and the chore of unloading began. After eighty-seven trees, Tashi lost count and his arms began to ache. The pile of trees on the wharf seemed to be double the size of the pile on the boat. Joe left one last tree on deck and climbed to the wharf beside Tashi.

Pointing at the tree left behind Joe explained, "We've gotta take that tree to Sailors' Snug Harbor on Staten Island. Dad sends them a tree every year. Says that he might just wind up in that place and he wouldn't want to be without a Christmas tree. Sailor's Snug Harbor is the last port o' call for old sailors. It is a big, beautiful building where all the old sailors go to live when they can no longer go to sea. You'll see if you come with me. Now, we've gotta find us a dolly to haul these trees up to the street."

Joe ran away and returned a few minutes later pulling an old rusty cart.

"This will do. Just pile the trees on here and the two of us can pull 'er up the street."

Joe and Tashi piled Christmas trees onto the little cart. The pile was so big that Tashi feared the cart would topple but Joe kept handing him trees. Finally Joe said, "OK, our first load goes to old Dennis Reilly; he'll deliver them to his people uptown. He'll be up there waiting for me. He's always here when we arrive."

Sure enough, at the head of the pier was a scruffy old man with a pipe clenched in his teeth and wearing a silk top hat with a ragged overcoat that barely covered his broad stomach.

"Joey, m'boy, has you got m'trees? The ladies on Park Avenue are waiting for me. The parties are tomorrow night and they wants their trees. Ah, they smell good. Makes me feel like Christmas is on its way. Me gawd, boy, ye're a foot taller than last year. Slow down or you'll pass me by." Dennis reached out and patted Joe on the shoulder. "Who's your friend?" he asked pointing to Tashi.

"Hey, Dennis, this is Tashi. He's from Japan. We're going to get these trees out of here in short order. Glad to see you again." Joe saluted Dennis as he unloaded the trees into his delivery van. All at once Joe stopped and looked at Dennis.

"What happened to Lady Elizabeth? You've got a new horse. Please, don't say the Lady died."

"Naw, nothing like that. Me son is driving the Lady today. This is Darlin' Nan.

The horse whinnied almost as though she knew that Dennis was talking about her.

"I'm glad Lady Elizabeth is all right. I really like that horse." Joe patted Darlin' Nan and continued to move trees.

In an hour and a half, all of the trees were gone. Joe invited Tashi to come back to the boat to have some supper. Tashi followed him down the pier thinking how lucky this boy was to have a father who took him sailing, and to have a job where he knew people like Dennis in port. They jumped aboard the *Lewis R. French* and went below.

Captain Pease was heating something on the wood stove. It smelled wonderful to Tashi.

"What's to eat?" Joe asked his dad.

"I have a little piece of mackerel and some potatoes in the pot. It'll be ready in no time. Did you sell all of the trees? How much did you make?" Captain Pease asked Joe.

Joe handed a fist full of dollar bills to his father. "Here's the money. Tashi was a big help. You owe him a day's wages. Why don't you ask him to help me get the tree to Snug Harbor? I know he'd like to come with me. Wouldn't you, Tashi?"

Tashi nodded his head in agreement.

The boys gobbled the fish stew. Joe looked at his father.

"Do you want Tashi to go with me to Staten Island?"

"Yep, I have to unload the rest of the lumber. If he wants, he can go with you. Remember to give my regards to Captain Ball and come right back. I may have a surprise for you when you return. Tashi, funny name. How'd you get here?" Captain Pease shifted all of his attention to Tashi.

"My real name is Takashi. The sailors on the *Sindia* called me 'Tashi'. I sailed from Kobe, Japan, round the Horn. Our ship wrecked in New Jersey in a terrible storm. Our captain lost his ship, the *Sindia,* even though no one died in the wreck. Today most of the crew sailed to England on the ship, *Georgian*. I want to sail on a ship to Japan, not to England. I work hard. I want to go home. Can you sail me home?" Tashi asked Captain Pease.

"Oh my, that's a good one. This old schooner likes to be in sight of land. We only coast the trip from Maine to New York. Of course, truth is, the *French* could sail around the world but it would be pretty uncomfortable at times. She was built for shallow waters, to coast over the waves and deliver freight. Ocean-going vessels, downeasters, are built to cut through the waves. I know lots of vessels from Maine that sail to Japan. I think Captain Sweetser is headed out to Japan after Christmas. You have quite a story, boy. Shipwrecked half way round the world. Hey, Joe, you have a long way to go to catch up with your new friend. He's a Cape Horner. Now, you boys better get going."

Tashi and Joe went down Front Street toward Battery Park and approached the ferry to Staten Island. They carried the Christmas tree over their heads and smiled at all of the people along the way who called out "Merry Christmas, boys."

In the bright sunlight of the early afternoon, traffic on South Street was unusually quiet but there were still enough horses and carts to kick up the dirty slushy snow and splatter the boys and their tree. Smells from the Fulton Fish Market made Joe wrinkle his nose.

"Whew, what a stink! Can you smell all the dead fish, Tashi? Just imagine how it smells on a hot summer day."

The boys walked a little faster. The collection of wild cats that hung around the waterfront were lounging on the steps of the buildings, on bins in the alleys, all sleek and well fed and enjoying the heat from the warm winter sun.

"I see so many cats," said Tashi. "It is like this at the wharf in Kobe. Those lazy cats know where the fish are caught. I saved Captain McKenzie's cat when the *Sindia* was wrecked. His name was Chauncey. Funny name for a cat!"

"You saved the captain's cat! You're a regular hero! Have to tell my Mom. She's the cat lover in our family." Joe gave Tashi a grin through the branches of the green tree.

They trudged down Front Street past the dark red brick buildings of the commercial district on their right hand side and the forest of tall masts of the huge ships in dock on their left. New York Harbor was a busy place. There were steamships in port from all over the world. Tugboats plied the river, taking boats to their places at the wharf and towing them out to sea.

There were so many ships that you had to make an appointment with a tug to get in and out of the harbor.

Tashi could now see that the *Lewis R. French* was one of the smallest vessels in port. It was also obvious that there were more steamships in port than sailing ships. In Japan it was the other way round.

"I can see the ferry dock!" yelled Joe, and he gave a little tug on the tree almost causing Tashi to fall. "There it is! The Staten Island Ferry. Let's go!"

They stood the tree upright and shook off as much dirty snow and debris as they could. Then both boys got on the same side of the tree, with Tashi in the rear, as they headed up the gangplank on the ferry.

"Hey there, where do you think you are going with that Christmas tree?" the deck hand called out to them.

"We're taking this tree to the old sailors at Snug Harbor," answered Joe with a big smile.

"Oh, lads, what a lovely thing to do. Just let me show you where to stand the tree while we make our crossing. Wouldn't want anything to happen to the old sailors' Christmas tree, now would we?"

The deck hand led them to a space under the stairs to the second deck.

"Here you go. Just put it here and don't forget to take it with you when you get off on Staten Island." He chuckled as if he'd told a funny joke.

"Thank you, sir. This is a fine place and don't worry we'll not forget it," said Joe with a grin.

"Same thing happens every year. We get stopped carrying our tree aboard the ferry and the minute we say that it is for the old sailors we get treated like kings. Every man on every boat respects the old sailors. Come on, Tashi, let's head on up to the bow."

Joe scampered forward with Tashi following. They climbed the stairs to the upper deck and headed to the bow.

"Look at that, Tashi," Joe pointed to the city. "See that tall building? It's called the Flatiron building because of its shape, like your mother's iron. It is almost finished. I hope I can go to the top sometime." Twirling around Joe pointed, "Look there, the Statue of Liberty. Wish we had time and I'd take you there so we could walk around her crown. You can see so far from the top of the statue."

Tashi looked and looked. He could see the structure of the tall building that Joe called that funny name, the Flatiron Building. Behind him he could see the dull green statue of a woman holding a torch in her hand towering over the harbor on her tiny island. New York Harbor was suddenly a wonderful place to be.

With a shudder, the ferry left the dock and headed across the river to Staten Island. The thicket of masts on the sailing ships stuck up over the tops of the steamers in port. Noise mingled with the smells of crates of cargo from different countries around the world overpowering the salt breeze coming in from the ocean. Vibration and noise from the engine silenced Joe. He and Tashi walked around and watched the shore of one side of the river diminish as the other became larger. Tashi had never been on a steam ship and the noise disturbed him. The rumbling motion of the ferry was not as good as that of a square-sailed ship. He was glad he did not have to sail all the way to Japan on this ferry.

With a thud the ferry docked in Staten Island. "Come on, Tashi, gotta get the tree and hike up the hill to Snug Harbor. It is a long walk. Captain Ball always gives me a nickel to take the trolley back to the wharf. I bet he will give you one too. Let's go!"

The boys shouldered the tree with Joe leading the way down the gangplank and on to the cobblestones of the street. Tashi had so much greenery in his face that he could barely see where they were going. It was damp and cold but Joe kept up the pace so that both boys were warm enough.

"We're almost there," Joe told his friend. "I can see it now."

They walked along Front Street and approached a big iron gate. The big dome of a building with its columned porch shone bright in the red afternoon sun.

"This year's Christmas tree, I see," remarked the gatekeeper. "You know where to go. So go right in. Merry Christmas, Joe."

"Merry Christmas," replied Joe, as he led Tashi and the tree up the long drive to the front door of the beautiful building. At the front door, they leaned the tree against the wall, rang the bell and went in. "We will leave the tree here and go pay our respects to Captain Ball. He is from Searsport, Maine. He knew my grandfather."

Tashi and Joe entered the building. They greeted all of the old men sitting in their chairs smoking their pipes and enjoying the fire in the huge fireplace. One old man got up and walked towards them.

"Aye, Joe, I've been expecting you. Who is your friend?" he said.

"Captain Ball, this is my friend Tashi. He was shipwrecked in New Jersey and now he's looking for a ship to take him home to Japan. Dad thinks that maybe he can sail out east with Captain Sweetser in the New Year. How are you? Your tree is on the front porch. Merry Christmas!" Joe sputtered out the words.

"Not so fast my boy. I'm fine. Japan eh? I've been to Kobe many times. What's that bloody earring?" he asked, pointing to Tashi's golden earring. "Did you sail round the Horn?"

Tashi looked at the old man and replied, "We sailed round the Horn and then grounded the *Sindia* on the beach in New Jersey. Now, I want to go home."

"You stay with Joe and Captain Pease. They will find you a berth on a downeaster, no better vessels on the sea. The Maine captains are good men. You can trust Captain Pease and it looks like you and Joe are great friends. Good for you, son."

"Captain Ball, we've gotta go now. Gotta sail home in the morning. Ma will be expecting us for Christmas." Joe looked at the Captain with a grin.

"Thank you for the Christmas tree. That wonderful scent makes me think of Maine. Here's a nickel for you and a nickel for Tashi to take the trolley back to the ferry. Here is another nickel. Treat yourselves to some roasted chestnuts on the way. Regards to Cap'n Pease and your family." He walked with the boys to the door and waved as they walked away. "Merry Christmas."

Tashi and Joe ran to the ferry. They decided to save their nickels for a treat later on.

"Let's go, Tashi. Must get back to the *French* and get ready to leave in the morning. You will come home with us, won't you? Dad will find you a way home and I want to know what his surprise is, don't you?"

Tashi was trying hard to keep up with Joe, who talked so fast and jumped from topic to topic in seconds. This had been an exciting day. Tashi wanted to go home; he just knew Captain Pease would help him.

Chapter 3

Aboard the *Lewis R. French*

THE CITY LIGHTS OF NEW YORK SPARKLED in the twilight as the ferry chugged across the East River. Tashi was reminded of his own seaport town, Kobe, but it did not shine as brightly after dark. The United States had magical electric lights that turned on with a switch. The lights in Kobe were mostly lamps filled with oil that came to port on vessels like the Sindia. Tashi and Joe were quiet on the trip across the river, comfortable in their new friendship.

"Joe, where do we sail in the morning?" asked Tashi.

"So, you are gonna come with us, Tashi. Good!" said Joe. "We are sailing to Searsport, Maine. My mother and little brother, Billy, will be waiting for us."

"How many days?" Tashi was curious.

"Three days of sailing if the wind comes from the west, and four if we have to sail into the wind. It takes a little doing but we will be OK. Dad is ready to go." Joe said.

A sudden shiver of the deck and the ferry nudged the dock. With squeaking and a slow whine the gate was let down and the passengers disembarked. Joe and Tashi were the last to leave as they had to climb down from the bow of the upper deck.

"Let's go!"

They ran down Front Street toward Pier 16 and the Lewis R. French tied at dock. There was a warm glow from all of the portholes as the boys climbed aboard over the gunwale.

"Dad, Cap'n Ball sends you his greeting. He was happy to get the tree. What's the surprise?" Joe talked so fast that Tashi had to work hard to understand, and didn't get every word.

"Slow down, son. You make me tired just listening to you Take off your jackets and have some dinner. We have to finish up this fish stew."

Captain Pease ladled out two mugs of stew and handed the boys big white square crackers to eat with it.

"Like this, Tashi," said Joe as he crumbled his crackers into the stew. "Makes it taste better and last longer if you put your crackers in the stew."

On the table was a big crate. Tashi looked at it and held back the tears. Black squiggly lines were painted all over the crate, Japanese characters. Tashi could read that it was addressed to New York City and that the package had been packed in Japan. Tashi read the characters that said the box contained some kind of dishes. Just looking at it made him homesick.

He waited for Captain Pease to speak.

"Well, Joe, here is the surprise. It's your mother's Christmas present. Would you like to see it?" He opened the box.

Captain Pease pulled out small objects wrapped in squares of white rice paper. He unwrapped one and it was a perfect little teacup painted with cherry blossoms and a beautiful woman sitting in the garden.

"It is geisha," whispered Tashi.

"What is a geisha?" asked Joe.

"Tell him, Tashi," said Captain Pease quietly.

"Geisha are beautiful women who make tea and happiness," replied Tashi with a tear sliding down his cheek. He wanted to go home, and seeing all of this beautiful Japanese porcelain made that feeling even stronger.

Captain Pease unwrapped six cups and six saucers, a sugar pot, cream pitcher and a squatty round teapot with a bamboo handle. All of the dishes had golden rims and were painted with flowers in gardens, with beautiful women gracing every piece.

Joe looked at his friend, "What's the matter, Tashi? Don't you like the dishes? I think they are beautiful."

"I look at the beautiful dishes and am sad. I want to go home."

His sad eyes looked at Captain Pease as the words were spoken.

"Tashi, we will get you on a downeaster sailing east. I promise. Now, you just stop worrying and come home with us for our family celebration. After Christmas we will find you a ship. Boys, we have some work to do before we turn in. I have all of the crates of china aboard but they must be stowed away."

Captain Pease led Tashi and Joe out on deck where stacks of wooden boxes covered the bulkhead. Every box was painted with black Japanese calligraphy. Tashi looked at the boxes and felt a wave of memories flood over him. He had spent many happy hours with his aunt and brother practicing forming the many characters with his brush. Seeing these boxes covered with Japanese writing symbolized the beginning of his journey home.

He and Joe took turns carrying the boxes below through the narrow companionway to the area where the captain wanted them secured. It took some time but the boys finished in time to hear, "Tea kettle is on and there are a few of your Mother's molasses cookies left. We will sail at dawn."

Joe and Tashi happily sipped their tea and Tashi greedily ate the big brown cookie that Captain Pease handed to him.

"Flood tide in the East River is at 6:15 a.m. It will be dark but the sun will rise soon. We can warp the *French* to the end of the pier and the tide will carry us through Hell's Gate into Long Island Sound. If this wind holds, we'll be on a reach and make good time. Cross your fingers, boys, that the wind holds. Time to catch some shut-eye."

Captain Pease opened his Bible to read by the kerosene lamp that lit the main cabin of the boat. Joe motioned to Tashi, and they left for the forward cabin, where Joe stowed his things.

"You take the bottom bunk, Tashi. I'm used to the top one. Here's a blanket for you."

Joe handed Tashi a white wool blanket with red, black, green and yellow stripes at one end.

"Thank you. I sleep fine in bottom bunk. I sleep on deck on the *Sindia*. This is much better."

Tashi stowed his duffle at the foot of his bunk. The bag was almost empty but did contain his precious half-model of the *Sindia*. Tashi took the warm wool blanket and curled up on the lower bunk and was asleep before Joe had his head on his pillow.

Chapter 4

To Maine

"COME ON BOYS! RISE AND SHINE." Captain Pease roused Joe and Tashi out of their bunks.

"Ah, Dad, it's cold!" complained Joe.

"Let's go! It will be warm enough when the sun rises."

In the cold black darkness of early morning, Joe and Tashi climbed out of their bunks. Neither had taken off their clothes the night before, so they were ready to go. Tashi carefully folded his warm wool blanket and stowed it under the lower bunk. Joe left his in a muddle and frowned as he watched Tashi tidy his bunk.

"Don't be too neat or you'll have my dad yelling at me" he muttered and gave Tashi a big smile.

Tashi could smell the coffee brewing and he wished it were tea. No point in fussing about it. He'd drink the warm coffee with lots of sweet canned milk and sugar in it and wait to see what else would be served for breakfast. After all of the strange things he had eaten aboard the *Sindia* he was ready to eat anything when he got hungry. Good thing his brother Sami wasn't here because he was really particular about what he ate and would never drink coffee.

"The flood tide will be running full speed in about thirty minutes. We have to be ready to go by then. We're in luck. There's a westerly blowing about twelve knots that will carry us right up the East River. I'll take the helm for the first leg and then, Joe, you will take your turn. Tashi, you'll be our lookout. When we get to open water I'll teach you to steer. By the time we get to Searsport, I'll make a real helmsman out of you." Captain Pease sounded happy to be heading home.

"Joe, you get the bow-line and walk us down the pier."

With that, Joe jumped from boat onto the dock. He let go the two spring lines that kept the schooner from sliding back and forth in the wake of ships passing and his father hauled them aboard.

"Tashi, you get on the dock and handle the stern line."

Tashi jumped to the pier. Joe tugged on the bowline and began to pull the *French* to the end of Pier 16. Tashi followed along, holding the line tightly, carefully controlling the stern of the boat. When the boat reached the end of the pier Joe looped the bowline around a cleat and tossed the bitter end aboard to Captain Pease. Joe started down the pier to help his friend with the stern line. But his time aboard the *Sindia* had made Tashi a quick learner and he had already made a turn on a cleat and was ready to toss the bitter end to the captain. The *French* was now held bow and stern alongside the pier with loops of line that could be released from on-board. It was now time to raise the mainsail.

The boys jumped aboard.

Captain Pease gave the order.

"Let the sheet run free and we'll raise the mainsail." The *French* was a gaff-rigged topsail schooner. The mainsail was raised by hauling up the wooden gaff attached to the top edge of the sail. Separate halyards controlled the two ends of the gaff, the peak and the throat. The boys handled the throat halyard, Captain Pease the peak. Raising the mainsail was a team effort. Hand over hand they pulled on the coarse manila halyards putting all of their weight into the effort. Slowly the huge, white sail unfurled and fluttered in the breeze.

"Half way there!" Captain Pease called out and Joe laughed. It seemed that this was his father's little joke. More hauling on the halyards. More fluttering sail.

"Half way there!" Captain Pease repeated. This time both boys laughed out loud.

Finally the captain announced, "Good job. Make 'em fast, Joe."

Joe tied off the halyards to the pins at the base of the mast and coiled the excess line neatly.

"Now boys, up with the foresail."

Joe and Tashi raised the foresail just as they had raised the mainsail, and Joe quickly tied off the foresail halyards.

"OK boys, the plan is to release the stern line first and then the bow line. The wind will blow us off the dock. Then we'll trim in the sheets and be underway. Tashi, you can haul in the stern line now. Joe, get ready to let go the bow." Captain Pease was all business as he gave the orders to his two boys.

"Aye, aye, captain." Joe and Tashi did exactly as ordered. They released the boat from its safe berth at the pier, and watched the sails fill with wind as the boat inched out into the East River.

Captain Pease headed her north on the river.

"Okay boys, let's raise the headsails and get her going. We're going home for Christmas."

"Come on, Tashi. Let's do it." Joe spoke carefully to his friend.

Tashi followed along, knowing how important it was to do exactly what he was told for he, Joe and Captain Pease had to work together to make this boat sail. He took the end of the line Joe handed to him and again they pulled hand over hand. The big white jib went sliding up the forestay. Then they quickly raised the forestaysail.

"Make fast," ordered Captain Pease, and Joe cleated the halyards.

"Haul in on the sheets," the captain said.

Joe and Tashi adjusted the sheets and felt the boat surge as the wind filled the sails and the current of the river helped them go toward home.

"Let's get her under the bridge and you can make us some breakfast, Joe."

The boys looked up from their tasks and saw the Brooklyn Bridge in all her glory. The dark gray Maine granite glistened in the early morning light, casting shadows on the water where they sailed in the dusky grey dawn. The bridge was so big. Their boat seemed so small. As they went under the bridge, Tashi turned around to take one last look at Manhattan Island. In the far distance he could see the Statue of Liberty.

A ferry crossed the river astern going to Staten Island. It was the same ferry that he and Joe had taken yesterday. The lights of the city were twinkling and the misty dawn was turning to a golden glow. The sun would shine bright on their first day aboard the *Lewis R. French*. Tashi tried to remember everything. He wanted to tell the stories to his brother, Sami, when he returned to Kobe. He knew that Sami would believe him, but he wasn't sure that Uncle Hiroshi and Aunt Lei would.

"Joe, you can get started on breakfast. Tashi, you get on the bow with a boat hook and fend off anything that is floating in the river. We need to be

very careful of floating debris until we get through Hell Gate."

"What is Hell Gate?" asked Tashi.

"It's where the Harlem River flows into the East River, and the two currents are powerfully vicious. Ships have been known to turn around in their whirl. It's a scary passage but it ain't nothing compared to Cape Horn, Tashi. You've sailed the worst."

Tashi smiled and fingered the gold earring in his ear. It was still a little tender but he was proud to wear it.

"Wonder what Mother will say when we bring home a heathen Japanese with a bloody earring in his ear?" Joe howled.

His father heard his comment and said, "Watch your words, Joe! Your mother will be proud to have such a brave young sailor in her home."

"I'll tell Mother about Tashi rescuing the captain's cat when the *Sindia* wrecked and that will impress her more than him sailing round Cape Horn," laughed Joe and he headed to the galley to fix a little breakfast for his father and friend.

The passage up the East River into Long Island Sound was perfect: good wind, a fair tide and little traffic on the river. Tashi was standing on the bow watching for debris, in this strong current they did not want anything hitting them, or the *French* hitting anything in the water, Captain Pease waited for some breakfast. He had bought a fresh loaf of bread at the market in New York, and there was a tin of peaches to be opened. A wheel of cheddar from England was wrapped in damp cloth and ready to be eaten. There would be little hot food for the next few days except for the hearty stew that was always aboard. Captain Pease liked to eat and was a good cook. None of his hands ever complained about the food. Joe took Tashi a piece of bread and cheese and told him that he could eat more later.

Tashi and Joe had their chores to do. They washed the decks and made sure all lines were coiled and stowed out of the way. They polished the brasses with bits of cotton wool. The sun was beating against the dark shiny green paint of the cabin top making it warm enough for them to warm their hands. Soon it was Joe's turn at the wheel.

"Hold her steady. That will keep us reaching and making good way," said Captain Pease. "We don't want to miss Christmas."

Joe showed Tashi how to steer the boat so that the needle of the compass would stay right where the captain had ordered. It seemed impossible that the big boat could be sailing in the right direction by just maintaining the needle position on the compass face. Tashi knew about charting and compasses, but he had never been permitted to touch the wheel on the *Sindia.* He could see that if Joe turned the wheel to starboard the boat turned to the right and the compass needle moved. If he turned the wheel to port the reverse occurred. It was a constant tweaking of the wheel to maintain the course. Joe concentrated and paid attention to his task.

Soon they could see the lighthouse at Montauk Point far in the distance.

"Tashi, come here!" the captain called.

Tashi went down the companionway into the saloon, where Captain Pease had the chart spread out on the table. He pointed to New York and then northeast to Maine.

"Right here on Penobscot Bay is where we are headed. We will pass Connecticut to port and Long Island to starboard before we sail into the Atlantic Ocean. See this little island, Block Island," he pointed to the chart. "We will go west of the island and sail on to Cape Cod. See there, it looks like a fish hook and we've got to go around it. There's been talk about digging a canal through right here," and he pointed to the base of the peninsula, "but nothing has happened. When we get around Cape Cod we're half way home. If this wind holds we will be there early on the day before Christmas Eve." Captain Pease spoke to Tashi as if he knew the boy could read a chart.

Tashi said not a word.

"Have you ever seen a chart, boy?"

Now he had to answer.

"Yes, Captain Pease. I learned to read chart on the *Sindia.* Captain MacKenzie helped me read the charts. I want to be captain some day."

Captain Pease chuckled. "You've got a good start. Sailing round the Horn before you're shaving your whiskers. I fancy you will be a good captain someday."

The west wind held and they sailed on day and night for three days until they saw the light blinking at Matinicus Rock and the *Lewis R. French* headed for Penobscot Bay like a horse headed to the barn.

"I see the light, we're on our way home, boys," said Captain Pease.

In the light of dawn the sky was glowing pink and gold. The lighthouse beacon was a welcoming sight. Joe and Tashi leaned against the main cabin and watched the sun rise over the dark blue sea aft of the schooner. The morning was clear and crisp and the air cold. Everyone aboard was hoping the good weather would hold until they were safe at dock in Searsport, Maine.

"Hey, Tashi, over there is Mantinicus Rock. Puffins live on that island. They are the funniest little birds. Sad to say, they aren't there now. It's winter now and they're all off-shore feeding. Nobody knows where they go in the winter and they always come back to their home on this island. Sort of like you, Tashi, nobody at home knows where you've gone and you want to go home." Saying that Joe scrambled below and came back with a book and a spyglass.

“Here Tashi, take a look.” Joe handed Tashi the spyglass.

Through the lens Tashi could see the little island, spotty with snow.

“No trees on the island so the little birds have to live in burrows in the ground. Can’t see the burrows because of the snow.” Joe told Tashi while paging through his book. “Here’s what they look like. Joe pointed to a picture of a little black and white bird with a big orange bill.

Tashi said, “I know those birds.”

“You do? How can you?”

“Birds just like that live in Japan. Aunt Lei has painted them on cups and plates. I wish I could see them here,” replied Tashi as he held the spyglass to his eye and stared at the island.

“No chance of that. They only live on islands in the spring and summer. In the springtime, I watch for them as we sail into the bay. Spotting the puffins in the spring is my welcome to Maine.”

“I wonder if your puffins can fly all the way to Japan?” mused Tashi.

"I wonder," replied Joe.

Tashi thought about the little birds. When he returned to Japan he would find out about them. In the meantime, he stared at the drawing in the book memorizing their color, the shape of their big orange bills and every detail of the little birds. Tashi leafed through the book. In it, he saw drawings of other birds that were familiar to him. There were pictures of the big grey birds with long legs that he often saw in Japan. He had seen those long~legged grey birds wading in the water along the shore in this new place. The white birds flying overhead that Joe called seagulls were everywhere in Japan. It was as if his friends, the birds, had followed him on his journey.

Aunt Lei would know if their birds were the same as these birds. She could identify all the birds they saw at home. It was a strange time for Tashi. He knew Aunt Lei would love to see the birds in Maine. She would say that seeing familiar birds was a happy way to start the day.

hatch to the boys standing in the fog shivering with drops of salty water streaming down their oilskins.

"Thanks, Father. Eat fast, Tashi, or it will get cold." Joe dug in. Tashi marveled at the speed with which Joe could eat a meal. His breakfast disappeared before Tashi had eaten half of his. Bacon and eggs were a treat, and both boys were happy to have a little fog so they could have this good breakfast.

Tashi took the plates below. He helped Captain Pease clean up the galley and get the cabin in order. There was no slacking off on a sailing schooner even if the fog had them stopped. They stowed the dishes and folded the towels and cleaned the cabin. With both of them working it didn't take too long.

"Father, it's lifting," came Joe's voice down the hatch.

Sure enough, the fog was thinner and glimpses of shore were could be seen through the mist. Bobbing in the water were colored floats that belonged to lobstermen marking their lobster pots at the bottom of the bay.

"Joe, what are those colored things floating in the water?" asked Tashi.

Joe explained lobstering to Tashi. Traps were set to catch the lobsters on the bottom. A line with a colored float attached floated on the surface of the water and marked the traps. The lobstermen had to haul the traps up on the stern of their boats to see if they had caught a lobster. It was hard, cold work, but lots of men in Maine did it to provide lobster to the fancy people in New York and Boston who loved to eat the creatures. Each lobsterman had his own colors on the floats. Tashi knew they were getting close to port when they saw the lobster buoys.

"Don't know who has the yellow buoys," said Joe. "Look for the orange and green ones, they belong to my Uncle Fred. When we see them, we will almost be home."

Captain Pease took the helm. Joe went to his look out position with Tashi at his elbow, watching the shoreline slide along like a snake in the grass. Once in a while smoke drifted in the air from a fireplace in a farmhouse. The smell wafted out across the water mingling with the salt of the sea. Tashi watched the white bubbly foam of the bowspray and the bowsprit bob up and down as they cut through the dark blue water. The sun from aft the boat made a mirror of the water and a shaky image of the boat was reflected on its surface. A glorious day emerged as they progressed up Penobscot Bay, passing a few villages and islands.

"I can see the church steeple. We're home! There it is, Searsport. See the church and the houses?" Joe cried out excitedly.

In the distance Tashi spied white houses and a church steeple standing tall and straight over all. On the port side there was a big ship on the land resting in a huge cradle. They must build ships in Searsport, he thought. It was a tiny village, not at all like Kobe which stretched for miles beyond the waterfront. They could see where this little village ended and the farmland began.

"Prepare to lower sail." Captain Pease ordered.

Joe and Tashi took their stand by the mainmast where the halyards of the mainsail were fastened. Captain Pease turned into the wind to take the pressure off the sail and the boys unfastened the line and slowly lowered the sails, controlling the halyards as they did so. He turned off the wind and they coasted on bare poles — no sails — right up to the wharf, where welcoming hands were waiting to help.

"Ayah, captain, we've been watching for you," said the man on the wharf. "Ye've had good weather these last four days. Got home just in time. Air feels like snow's coming."

"Thanks, Ed. Let's hope the snow holds off until we unload this boat. Got the Christmas presents for half the ladies of Searsport aboard." Captain Pease chuckled.

They tied the *French* to the town dock. More men walked out to greet them. Joe tried to look important as he threw lines to the waiting hands and issued orders as to how to tie her up. Tashi quietly did as he was told. The boat rested comfortably in dock.

"Joe, get Mother's present and take it home. I'll see to the off-loading of the boxes." While Captain Pease was busy with his task, Joe and Tashi tied a rope around the wooden box of dishes so they could carry it between them. The packed their gear in their duffles and put them on the dock. Mrs. Pease's box was put ashore separated from the other boxes.

"Let's go, Tashi. Mother and Billy will be waiting for us."

The boys picked up their burden and headed down the dock to the town. The walked up the cobblestone street past white houses festooned with pine boughs and defined by white picket fences. At the top of the hill, they could see a figure running and waving his arms.

"Joe, Joe... you're home!" a voice called out.

"It's Billy. Look, Tashi, it's my brother."

As the figure approached it became clear that the small boy wore a knitted cap that fell to his shoulders. Blue eyes sparkled under a fringe of blonde hair and a million freckles dotted his nose and cheeks. He threw his arms around his big brother's chest and said, "I was afraid that you and Dad weren't going to be here for Christmas."

Then he looked at Tashi. Billy stared at a strange face and noted the slanted black eyes of this boy taller than he, wearing a sweater and tattered pea coat much too big for him. He stared at the gold earring in his left ear.

"Who are you?" he said.

"Whoa, Billy, slow down. This is my new friend, Tashi. He is coming home with us for a while. Father has promised to find him a ship sailing to Japan so he can go home. Come on, we're headed home."

Joe, Tashi and Billy continued up the hill. They were a rag tag threesome in the cold morning. Little Billy in his red hat, Joe wearing his sailor's pea coat the tallest of the three, and dark-haired Tashi with a duffle bag over his shoulder.

They opened the gate to a little house with dormer windows and blue shutters and walked around the back to the kitchen door.

"Mother, I'm home!" shouted Joe.

A woman, her black curly hair escaping the bun at the nape of her neck, came to the door and hugged Joe.

"Look who's here? Welcome home, son. Where's your dad?"

"He and Ed are off-loading the cartons. He'll be along," replied Joe. "Mother this is Tashi. He has sailed around Cape Horn and that is why he has an earring. His ship wrecked in New Jersey and he saved the captain's cat. Now he wants to go home to Japan and Dad has promised to find him a berth on a downeaster. He will be here for Christmas." Joe rambled on while his mother took in the cut of Tashi's sails and quietly observed this new face in her kitchen.

"Welcome, Tashi. I bet you are hungry. Come on in." She led the boys into the kitchen.

Tashi looked around. Houses in America were very different from houses in Japan. Here there was so much confusion. Chairs and tables, pictures on the wall, and so many dishes sitting on the tables and stacked in glass front cabinets. Tashi was not used to sitting on chairs. He was used to sitting on cushions on the floor but Americans did not do that. He watched Joe and Billy and did just what they did. They hung their coats on hooks inside the door and Tashi hung his sweater. Joe set the big box in a corner and put his bag atop it. Tashi did the same. Then they sat at the table while Mother poured glasses of milk and put a plate of cookies in front of them. Both boys ate and talked as Tashi sat and listened.

On a rug by the fireplace, a big black cat stretched, watching the boys. The cat stood up and walked over to the kitchen table. It walked right over to Tashi and rubbed its cold nose on his ankle and its back against his leg. Tashi reached down to stroke it.

"Look at that! Old Blackie likes you! She doesn't like anyone. I guess she knows that you like cats," said Billy.

"Boys, take your things upstairs and get washed up. Your father will be home for dinner soon and we have lots to do. Tashi, Joe will take you in with him and Billy. Just pull out the trundle for Billy and Tashi can have his bed." Mother shooed the boys upstairs.

Tashi and Joe took their bags upstairs. Billy was close behind. "What's in your bag, Tashi?" asked Billy.

"None of your business" replied Joe.

"Some clothes and my half- model of the *Sindia,"* answered Tashi.

"Let me see," said Billy.

"You're such a pest," said Joe.

Tashi took the half-model out of his bag and handed it to Billy. The younger boy accepted it carefully and turned it over in his hands, looking at every side of the polished model.

"I carved that on board. I want to take it home to Japan," said Tashi quietly.

"It's beautiful," said Billy.

"It really is," echoed Joe. They examined the half-model and handed it back to Tashi.

The boys stowed their gear, washed their faces and combed their hair and went downstairs to wait for Father to come home for dinner. Tashi liked this home that was warm and safe, with good smells of dinner cooking. He wondered what he would be eating this evening. Food in America was hard for him to understand. He tried everything and hoped he would like something. Eating strange food was part of this adventure.

It was dark when Captain Pease arrived for dinner. Baked beans and corn bread were favorites of all the Pease family, and they told Mother over and over how good the dinner was. Tashi ate his beans and bread, wishing for some rice and fish. He wondered what would be next and if he would always be hungry in this happy home.

After dinner Mother quietly asked Tashi, "Would you like a cup of tea?"

"Oh, please, thank you," replied the happy boy. Maybe there was hope for something good to eat; at least there would be tea.

"Joe, I think we should give Mother her present now. Don't you?" Captain Pease looked at Joe and pointed to the box in the corner of the room.

"Oh yes, Father," said Joe. "Come on, Tashi, help me with the box."

The boys placed the big box before Mrs. Pease.

"What is this? Do I get to open my Christmas present early?" Mrs. Pease, with much enthusiasm, accepted the big box, thanked them and immediately opened the lid. She took out the teacups and teapot and unwrapped them carefully, smoothing the squares of white rice paper that protected the dishes.

"Tashi, you recognize these dishes, don't you?" she asked. "I am so happy to have such beautiful dishes and a guest from Japan to drink tea with me. Thank you."

The whole family drank tea from the beautiful Japanese cups. Captain Pease announced that it was time for the boys to go to bed as they had lots to do the next day, Christmas Eve. Tashi had no idea what unusual surprises would come with Christmas Eve.

Chapter 6

Christmas Eve

"GET UP, TASHI," JOE WOKE HIS FRIEND. "It's the day before Christmas and we have lots to do."

Tashi opened his eyes and looked around. He wasn't sure where he was. Then he threw his legs over the side of the bed and stepped on little Billy.

"Whatcha doing?" cried Billy from his trundle bed low on the floor. The trundle bed slipped under the big bed when not in use. Anyone who slept in the little trundle ran the risk of being stepped on by the person in the big bed above.

"I'm sorry," said Tashi while Joe laughed at his little brother and his friend all tangled in the bedclothes.

The boys went down to the kitchen where captain and Mrs. Pease were drinking coffee and making plans. Breakfast porridge simmered on the stove and the boys helped themselves and sat down at the table.

"Good morning, boys," Captain Pease greeted the sleepy boys. "Are you ready to get some things done? We have to decorate our tree, wrap presents, and must be ready to go to church this evening. It is a big day and I'm glad you are here to help, Tashi."

Mrs. Pease got up and went to the sink to start the dishes.

Captain Pease walked out to the back porch and dragged in a fir tree. He proceeded to nail a cross of wood to the bottom of its trunk, which would allow the tree to stand upright, and then took the tree into the living room and positioned it in front of the bay window. Billy and Joe tagged along chattering about popcorn and cranberries and boxes of ornaments. This tree looked like the tree that Tashi and Joe had taken to Captain Ball in New York. Tashi thought it a very strange custom to bring trees into the house.

"Tashi, have you ever decorated a Christmas tree?" asked Joe.

"No, never," replied Tashi.

"Well, come on. The ornaments are in the attic." With that Joe headed up the stairs and Tashi followed. Cold air blew past them as they entered the narrow door that led to an area under the roof. A box labeled "Christmas" sat at the head of the stairs. Joe picked it up and carried it back to the living room where the tree stood by the front window looking out to the street.

"We hang all the ornaments on the tree now. Later on, before we go to church, Dad pops corn and we string it with cranberries to finish off the decorations. The tree always looks beautiful and it smells so good." Joe explained.

Glass balls sparkled and the other colored glass toys shone as Joe opened the box. The boys carefully hung the decorations on the tree with little silver hooks. Joe would stop and step back from the tree to look at it and then move the ornaments around until he was satisfied with their placement.

"Done," said Joe, and Mother agreed.

"It is a beautiful tree. Don't you think so, Tashi?" she asked. "Tashi, do you know about Christmas?"

"Oh yes, Mrs. Pease," replied Tashi, "I learned my English at the Christian church. They taught me all about baby Jesus. We sang songs too but we never had a Christmas tree."

Mrs. Pease chuckled.

"I think the Christmas tree is part of the celebration that started in Germany and probably just has not moved on to Japan. The important thing to remember is that we are celebrating the birth of Jesus and the rest is just a party. Is your family Christian, Tashi?" asked Mrs. Pease.

"My family believes in Buddha's teachings and in Jesus' teachings. In Japan, many people believe that both are leading to the path of truth," replied Tashi.

Mrs. Pease smiled and gave Tashi a hug.

Tashi shook his head, wondering what next? This tree trimming was bewildering, but lots of fun. He had more stories to tell his brother Sami. The Christmas tree story would make Sami laugh. He would never imagine a tree covered with glass balls and strings of popcorn standing in the living room.

After lunch, Captain Pease invited Tashi to walk down to the harbor with him while Mrs. Pease and the boys finished the Christmas preparations. On the way he spoke seriously.

"You know, boy," he said, "I have been asking around about passage for you back to the Far East. I think your best chance is to ship aboard a Downeaster on its way to deliver a cargo of case oil. We have lots of ships doing that. The problem is that most only go as far as Shanghai and you have to get to Kobe."

Tashi shivered with excitement. At last he would go home.

"Captain Pease, if I can get to Shanghai I can find my way to Kobe. Every day vessels from Shanghai sail into our harbor and off-load cargo at my Uncle's warehouse. I will find a way to Kobe even if I must stowaway."

"Well, Tashi, then I will proceed. I hear that Sewell's yard in Bath is finishing a bark for Standard Oil. She'll sail the first of the year. I know she will be headed for Shanghai. Let's see if my mates in the harbor know who has her helm."

Tashi and the captain walked on to the harbor with everyone along the way greeting Captain Pease with a "Good Morning" or "Merry Christmas". The sky was gray and the sun was hidden. The spirit of Christmas found its way into Tashi's heart. Captain Pease would find him a way to sail home!

Tree trimmed, dinner eaten, baths to be taken, the family readied themselves for Christmas Eve service at church. The Pease household took their baths in the kitchen once a week in an old galvanized tub. Mother heated some water poured it into the tub, left soap and towels on the chair and admonished Joe, "See to it that Billy is clean. I don't want to see any dirt behind his ears. Tashi, you can be first in the tub. The boys will wash up after you are finished. I've put your clean clothes on the sideboard."

Mother left the three boys in the kitchen calling, "Don't make a mess."

Much shivering and splashing and noise followed as the three boys bathed in the tub of soapy water. The kitchen was warm in front of the wood stove but really cold around the edges. Tashi and the boys hurried in and out of the tepid water.

Tashi dressed in the clothes that Mrs. Pease had left for him. New England housewives never discarded anything, and in the attic she had found Tashi worn clothes that fit him. As he dressed he wondered how the neighbors would receive him in church.

"Front and center! Inspection! Let's see how you look, boys."

Captain Pease waited for the boys to line up. He was dressed in his blue jacket with the brass buttons shining. The boys had on white shirts, blue trousers, hair combed and all three had warm wool peacoats. The coat Mrs. Pease had found for Tashi smelled of camphor just like the cargo on the *Sindia*.

Tashi stood straight and said, "Thank you for the clothes. My coat smells like the *Sindia*. The whole town of Ocean City, New Jersey, smelled like camphor oil when we ran aground. I will never forget the smell."

Billy and Joe giggled.

"We will be able to find you, Tashi, we can just follow our noses. You stink!"

"Don't worry Tashi, by the time we walk to church the smell will be almost gone. Let's go!" said the captain.

As they trudged through the snow up the

hill to the church, the church bells began to ring. Inside, almost the whole town of Searsport was gathered to sing Christmas carols and celebrate the holiday. Little candles twinkled as the Pease family and Tashi walked down the aisle to their seats in the third pew on the right side of the church. All eyes followed the small Japanese boy dressed in his navy coat with the candlelight making his gold earring sparkle. An undercurrent of quiet whispering filled the air as the family filed into their pew.

The pastor stood in his pulpit. The church became quiet and the beautiful tune of "Silent Night" played on the organ. Everyone then stood and sang the words that told the story of Christmas Eve. A hush came over the congregation after the last verse. The pastor opened his bible and read the Christmas story from the second chapter of Luke. He finished the reading with the words, "Glory be to God in the highest, and on earth, peace, good will toward men."

Tashi felt the peace of the moment. It was the same feeling of peace he felt when bowing before Buddha. In this church there were candles and singing. In his temple there was incense and chanting. Both places were sanctuaries of peace.

At the close of the service, Pastor Webb asked, "Have we any visitors here tonight?"

Captain Pease stood and pulled Tashi to his feet beside him.

"We have a visitor from Japan. His name is Tashi and he's looking for passage home. He sailed here with me and Joe aboard the *French* and I can vouch that he is a good worker. If any of the captains in the congregation are going to the Far East and need a cabin boy, he'd make a good one. Tashi's staying at my home. He has sailed around Cape Horn which is more than I've done, and I've been sailing all my life."

They took their seats. Tashi knew that everyone in the church was looking at him. He wondered what they were thinking and chuckled to himself. Some of these nice neighbors probably did not like seeing a young boy with a pierced ear any more than his Aunt Lei was going to like it. Too bad. He would tell his tale and then decide what to do about the earring.

After greeting all of their neighbors the family walked home. They took one last look at the Christmas tree in the parlor, festooned with strings of popcorn and cranberries, and went to bed.

Tashi could not sleep. This family was being so good to him and he wondered what he could do for them. The half model was all he owned and he wanted to take it to his family in Japan. Maybe he should give it to the Pease family. No, he knew what he could do. Carefully stepping over Billy in the trundle bed, Tashi crept down the creaking stairs into the kitchen. The moon was shining in the window and he could see well enough. On the sideboard were the little white squares of rice paper that had wrapped Mrs. Pease's dishes. He counted out twelve squares and sat down at the table. Fold, crease, fold. Tashi worked quietly. He thought about the many times that he and his brother had done this in Japan. Finished! On the kitchen table were twelve little birds folded into shape from the squares of rice paper. He gathered them into his shirttail and went into the living room. One by one he placed the small white birds on the branches of the Christmas tree.

Chapter 7

Christmas Day

"MERRY CHRISTMAS! MERRY CHRISTMAS!" Billy and Joe ran down the stairs yelling and whooping, "Merry Christmas!"

Tashi pulled on his pants and shirt and followed the two boys who were frolicking in the parlor in their nightshirts. Tashi laughed at the sight of the two white-clad figures dancing around the fancy tree in the midst of the formal parlor.

"Mother, look at the tree!" exclaimed Joe.

Mrs. Pease smiled walked over to the tree and picked up one of the little white birds that rested on the pine bough.

"Tashi, you were busy last night."

Surprised, the boys looked at their mother.

"What do you mean? Tashi was busy? Where would Tashi buy those white birds in the middle of the night?" Billy and Joe were puzzled.

"Tashi didn't buy these birds. He made them from paper with the ancient art of origami. Tashi knows what I mean. Thank you, Tashi."

She held the little bird for a minute and replaced it in the tree.

"Tashi, what is origami?" Joe asked.

"It is the art of folding paper. Aunt Lei shows my brother, Sami, and me how to fold. We make birds and flowers and boats by folding paper. Aunt Lei is an artist. She taught me and Sami the art of origami. I can show you how to fold a boat." Tashi was pleased that Mrs. Pease knew about origami.

"Let's eat breakfast. Then we will get dressed and open our presents. Tashi, you have given us a wonderful present and the birds will always be perched on our Christmas tree. Thank you."

Mrs. Pease smiled at Tashi, and they all followed her into the kitchen for breakfast.

Hot cakes eaten, Captain Pease announced, "Boys, get dressed and we will see what is in the packages under the tree."

"Ah, Father, we can open our presents now, why wait?" asked Billy.

"Get dressed!"

The boys went upstairs to dress. Tashi sat in the parlor with Captain and Mrs. Pease. He was pleased with the sight of his little white birds perched on the tree.

"Tell me about Aunt Lei," said Mrs. Pease.

"Aunt Lei is an artist. She paints on china. Her paintings of flowers and birds are known well in Kobe. She does not paint geisha girls on china, but she does teach geisha to paint. The geishas learn about painting and music and even origami. Aunt Lei tries to teach me and Sami how to paint. I try harder than Sami and I like to hear her stories. She will be happy to know that you like my birds on your Christmas tree." These were the most words that Tashi had spoken at one time. Mrs. Pease made him feel comfortable.

Under the tree were two boxes wrapped in tissue and tied with red ribbon.

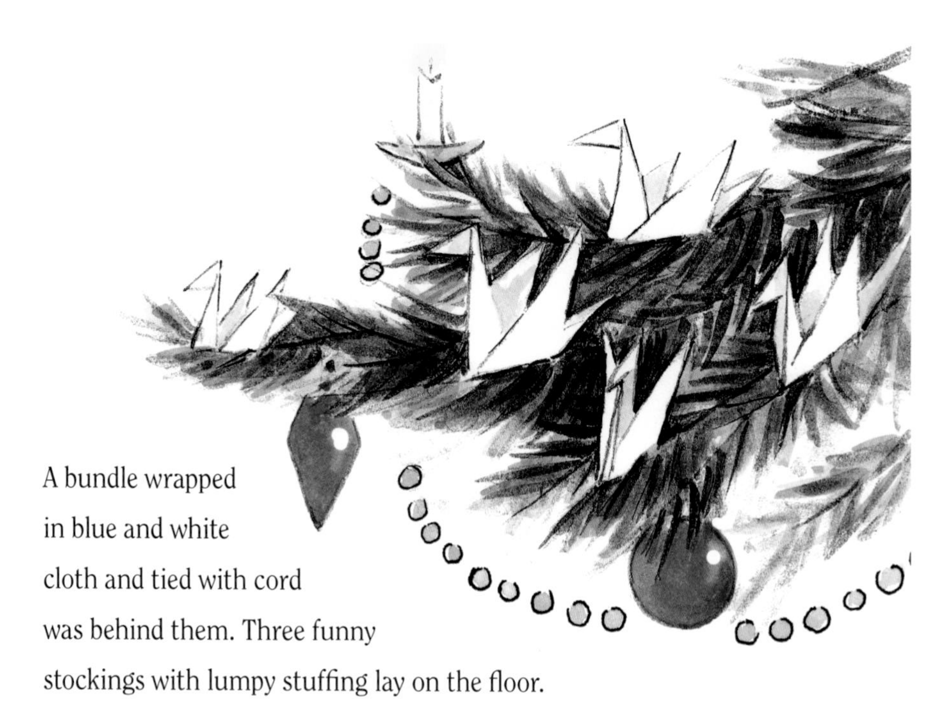

A bundle wrapped in blue and white cloth and tied with cord was behind them. Three funny stockings with lumpy stuffing lay on the floor.

Mrs. Pease left the room and returned when the boys came charging down the stairs.

"It's Christmas and I want to open my present!" Joe was too excited to wait.

"You're the oldest so you go first, Joe," announced Captain Pease.

Joe dived under the tree and looked at the cards on the three packages. The long skinny box was his. The bundle wrapped in cloth he gave to his father. The flat box with red ribbon went to Billy. Mrs. Pease put a small blue cloth covered box in Tashi's lap.

"We take turns opening our presents. I opened my beautiful Japanese tea set the other night so I was first. Now, Joe will open his, then Billy because he can't wait. After Billy you may open your box and Captain Pease is always last." Mrs. Pease explained the ritual to Tashi.

Joe tore the paper off his package and handed his mother the ribbon with a smile. Inside the box was a shiny brass spyglass.

"How wonderful! It's better than the one we have on board. Now I will really be able to see the puffins on the islands. Thank you." Joe swiveled his head around the room with the spyglass up to his eye.

Billy opened the flat box. It contained a Parcheesi game.

"Tashi can you play? I'll teach you. Thank you, Mother and Father, you know I wanted my own game." Billy opened the box to look at the game.

"Tashi, it's your turn," said Joe.

Tashi looked at the small blue box that rested on his lap. He took off the lid. There nestled in shiny red satin was a brush with a bamboo handle, a small foil-covered square, a little black dish, a blue and white brush rest and a small white saucer.

"Thank you. Thank you," said Tashi.

"What is it?" asked both boys.

"It is a painting set that Mrs. Evanson gave to me when she returned from Japan last year. I have no idea how to use it, but I think Tashi does. Don't you Tashi?" Mother inquired.

"Oh, yes! I will paint flowers and bamboo for you and will write names in Japanese." Tashi carefully replaced the lid on his box and held it to his heart.

"Now, I shall open my present," announced Captain Pease.

He looked at the cord, examined the blue and white fabric, turned it upside down and all around.

"Hurry, Father, we want to see what's inside." Joe was always impatient.

"I will take my time and enjoy it all," replied the captain, smiling. He untied the cord, carefully folded the fabric, and looked at the beautiful dark blue sweater inside. "Katherine, I am sure this took all of your spare time to knit and I think it is beautiful, thank you." He got out of his chair and walked over to Mrs. Pease and kissed her. The boys clapped and shouted "Merry Christmas".

"Let's take a look at our stockings."

There were three stockings all stuffed with walnuts and chocolates wrapped in paper. In the toe of each was a fat round orange. One was for Joe, one for Billy and the third one Joe handed to Tashi. The boys looked at all of the goodies and shoved them back in the stretched-out wool stockings.

"Come on Tashi, let's go into the kitchen and eat our oranges," exclaimed Joe.

"I want to save mine for tomorrow," said Billy. "Tashi, I want to see you paint."

The boys headed for the kitchen while Captain and Mrs. Pease enjoyed a moment of quiet on this Christmas morning. The sun was shining into the windows making sparkles from the reflection on the white snow. Captain Pease had shoveled the sidewalks before going to bed the night before. He knew that the neighbors would be coming to visit. They, too, would walk around the neighborhood with good Christmas wishes. It was the custom to go calling on Christmas day in Searsport, Maine.

Joe stood over the sink, dripping juice from his Christmas orange down his chin. Billy stood at Tashi's elbow watching him carefully place his brush on the table and the black pan at the top of the brush, the white dish to its right and then the little blue china thing under the brush propping the tip in the air.

"I need water and some paper," said Tashi.

"I'll get it," Billy grabbed what was left of the little white squares of paper on the sideboard, took a glass from the shelf, and, pushing Joe aside at the sink, filled it with water.

"Here you go, Tashi,"

Tashi unwrapped the little foil-covered square and placed it in the little black dish.

"What's that, Tashi?" questioned Billy.

"That is the ink stick. I make ink to paint with." He dipped the little square of ink in the water and rubbed it on the black dish. More water, more rubbing and then he picked up his brush. Dipping it in water and then into the ink, he sat with the brush poised over the paper and began to paint. In seconds he had painted a mountain with bamboo trees in the foreground bending in the wind. It was magic! With just a few strokes, he had a picture.

"Golly, Tashi, you are an artist. Look at this, Joe, and don't drip on his picture," Billy scolded his older brother.

"Do it again so I can see," said Joe.

Tashi rubbed some more ink and this time painted a little bird sitting on a branch with tiny little flowers on the branch. He made some marks in the lower left hand corner of the page.

"What's that?" asked Joe, pointing to the marks.

"That is my name. I can write your name, Joseph, but I don't know Billy." Tashi painted the symbols for Joseph on the page.

Now all three boys were sitting at the table. Tashi painted and painted. Joe and Billy were entranced. They were so involved in Tashi's painting that neither boy looked up when the kitchen door opened and Captain Pease followed by a man and two little girls came into the kitchen.

"Boys, Captain Sweetser is here with all of his family. Tashi I think you will want to meet him. He is sailing to Shanghai at the end of January," said Captain Pease.

Tashi looked up to see a stout man with a bald head and black whiskers. He put down his brush and stood.

"Captain Sweetser, this is the lad who wants to sail home to Japan. His name is Takashi, but we all use the nickname the sailors on the *Sindia* gave him — Tashi. So, this is Tashi and he would be a good cabin boy for you on your voyage. Let him work off his passage," announced Captain Pease.

"Look, Daddy, he is an artist. I wish I could paint like that," said one of the girls to her father.

"Tashi, I am glad to meet you and I do need a cabin boy. I see you are an artist but can you take orders and clean?" Captain Sweetser was stern but his eyes twinkled, and he held the hand of the smallest of the two sisters as she shyly looked at the Japanese boy.

"I can clean and take orders, Sir," replied Tashi.

"This is Clarabel and this little one is Susie," said Joe pointing to the two sisters. "Clarabel is in my class at school."

Clarabel sat down at the kitchen table to watch Tashi paint. She was all dolled up in her Christmas dress of red velvet and lace. She reached over to touch the black ink in the little white dish.

"Be careful, Missy," said Tashi, "don't spill the ink on your pretty dress."

"Pretty dress!" Joe chuckled. "Tashi likes Clarabel!" he taunted.

"Oh, Joe Pease you are such a tease," Clarabel retorted. "You couldn't paint like this if they tied you to the brush and table for ten years. Just be quiet!"

Tashi watched the girl out of the corner of his eye but kept right on painting flowers and bamboo with wispy leaves that he made with one swish of the brush. The small girl, Susie, stood behind him entranced. She placed her hand on the table by his and mimicked the motion of his brush strokes.

"I think I can do that," she said. "Please let me try."

Tashi stood up and gave her the brush. He showed her how to fill the brush with ink. She swished the brush to make some leaves and giggled as she did it. "Oh, Tashi, do you think you can teach me how to make the mountains, too? Do you know how to paint a pussy cat?"

"Susie, you are so silly. Tashi doesn't paint pussy cats," said Clarabel very seriously.

"I do," said Tashi and he picked up the brush and painted a cat with three or four swishes of the brush.

Clarabel and Susie watched in awe. Joe ate his orange and paid little attention to Tashi and the girls who were so absorbed in Tashi's painting.

"The girls and their mother are going to sail with me on this tour. They have never been "out east". When my wife sees this painting she will want to learn too. I hope I can get some work out of you other than painting," chuckled Captain Sweetser. "My bark is due to be launched in Bath early next month then we sail to the far east at the end of the month."

Mrs. Pease and Mrs. Sweetser crowded into the kitchen.

"My, look at the artist," said Mrs. Pease. "I came in to see if all of you would like some lunch?"

"Good idea," said Captain Pease, "join us for lunch."

The girls were nodding their heads *yes, yes!* It was agreed that the Sweetsers would stay for lunch with the family.

"Tashi, you will have to clean up the painting. You and the other children go in the parlor while I fix us some lunch. Mrs. Sweetser will keep me company. All of you, out of my kitchen," announced Mrs. Pease with a flourish.

Billy set up his Parcheesi game on the low table in the parlor. "Only four can play," said Billy. "What can we do? There are five of us."

The five children looked at each other, and Tashi admitted that he did not know how to play the game.

"That's fine, Tashi, you play with me and I will teach you how to play," said Clarabel. "It isn't hard and the two of us will surely win against this bunch."

Clarabel tossed her red curls and sat down next to Tashi ready to play.

"Red is my color," she announced and proceeded to pick up the red markers. "You can be yellow, Joe, Susie likes blue, which leaves the green for Billy." Clarabel passed out the markers.

"Wait a minute! It's my game," said Billy. "I declare! You are so bossy, Clarabel."

"Well, I am the champion Parcheesi player at our house," said Clarabel with a wicked little smile.

"Let's play," said Joe. "We'll see who wins this game."

The children played the game, and the two captains watched them and talked about their ships and the sea.

Tashi heard Captain Pease ask Captain Sweetser if he thought it was possible for him to take on Tashi as a cabin boy. Captain Sweetser told him that he was sure he could.

"Look at the boy. He is playing with our children as if he's known them all of his life. Isn't that strange? That boy is a survivor. He has learned how to make- do like a real Yankee. I like him. We'll get him home. His family must think him lost forever."

"We'll get Tashi fitted out to go with you," stated Captain Pease with great determination.

Tashi was silent listening to the children argue about Parcheesi and the captains planning the voyage. All he could think was *I'm going home.*

Chapter 8

The Astral

BLUE SKY OVERHEAD MADE THE LUMPY WATER of the Kennebec River shine like polished sapphires as Tashi and Joe stood in the bow of the French and watched the spectacle unfolding before them. A cold wind tousled their hair and rocked the schooner but the warm sun kept their shivers at bay. Captain Pease had decided that he and the boys — Joe, Billy and Tashi — would watch the launching of the *Astral* at Sewall's shipyard in Bath, Maine from the deck of their schooner. They packed Tashi's gear and boarded the *Lewis R. French* at dawn to sail down the Penobscot and up the Kennebec River for the launching, late in the afternoon of January 11, 1902.

Sitting on the cabin top of the French, tied to a mooring in the river, provided a great vantage point. The *Astral,* poised on greased skids, waited, ready to slide into the water. On a platform at the bow of the bark, high above the wharf, were assembled a group of important people including Captain and Mrs. Sweetser and Clarabel and Susie. Captain Sweetser was proud to be sailing on the *Astral*'s maiden voyage to the Far East for the

Standard Oil Company.

"I can see the lady with a bottle of champagne in her hand," exclaimed Joe, holding his new spyglass to his eye and training it on the dignitaries' platform. "Tashi, take a look!"

He handed the spyglass to his friend.

As Tashi looked through the spyglass, the lady swung the bottle of champagne like a baseball bat and hit the bow. The bottle exploded and he could see bubbles drip down the bow of the *Astral* and splash on the lady's fur coat.

"It's done! She's christened the *'Astral'*. Now, watch! Put down the glass, you must see the whole picture." Captain Pease took the spyglass from Tashi. He and the three boys watched as the shiny white bark, adorned with only a simple black stripe painted round her for decoration, slid down the greased rails into the river. The *Astral* had a steel hull, and the three hundred thirty-two feet of metal hit the water with a big splash, causing waves to echo across the harbor and rock the *French*. A loud cheer erupted from the crowd on the platform. Tashi, Joe and Billy joined in the cheers.

"Tashi, you're going to sail home on that ship. I wish I were going with you!" exclaimed Joe.

"Joe, time enough to sail around the world. Your mother would box your ears if she heard you say that." Captain Pease smiled as he looked at the three young boys. The fact that these two boys, born half way round the world from each other, had met and become friends in a world that each would probably sail around more than once was an occurrence that could only be called incredible.

As Tashi watched the action ashore he thought about all that had happened since Christmas day when he met Captain Sweetser. He'd learned

that there were more sea captains from Searsport than any other town in the United States. Captain Pease knew all of them. The captains lived in Searsport and many of the sailing vessels were built there. The ships in Searsport were built of wood. Steel barks like the *Astral* had to be built in Bath. Tashi and Joe had walked all around the small town of Searsport. They walked out to the end of the town pier and watched the men work on the huge wooden hulls of the sailing ships sitting in their cradles at the edge of the river.

Joe even took Tashi to school with him one day. Clarabel Sweetser was in Joe's class. They arrived early, before the teacher came into classroom.

When the boys entered the classroom, Clarabel took over and introduced Tashi to everyone as though he were her friend and not Joe's. Clarabel pulled down the map at the front of the classroom. The other children gathered round.

"Here's where we are in Searsport, Maine." She pointed to their place on the map. "And this is where we are going." With her finger she traced across the Atlantic Ocean down to the southern tip of Africa and headed north across the Indian Ocean.

"Now, this is the part I am not sure of because there are so many little islands in the way but I know we are headed to Shanghai up the Yangtze River. Tashi wants to go home to Kobe, Japan, which is right here." She pointed to the city marked on the map at the edge of the Inland Sea of Japan.

Tashi was impressed by her knowledge of geography. He also noted that when Clarabel had something to say everyone listened.

"Tashi told me that vessels sail from Shanghai to Kobe everyday," Joe chimed in. "If Captain Sweetser can sail Tashi to Shanghai that will be just fine. Tashi will find his way home from there. Guess you won't be sailing around Cape Horn, Clarabel. Too bad, I know you'd like an earring like Tashi's." Joe giggled and so did the other children.

"Joe Pease, you are such a show-off. I would never wear only one earring. Why, I'd look like a pirate," fumed Clarabel. "You are just jealous that you aren't coming with us. We are going to have an adventure. Aren't we Tashi?" She looked to Tashi to reply.

"We must sail very far for me to go home. When I get back to Kobe I will have sailed round the world." Tashi answered. Joe hung his head and walked to the back of the classroom and sat down. Tashi followed him.

"Clarabel thinks she knows everything. You'd better watch out for her or she will boss you around for the whole voyage," Joe grumbled to Tashi.

Later in the evening, Mrs. Pease pulled out an old sea bag and helped Tashi pack. She gave him a set of oilskins to keep him dry in rough weather. He had two pairs of pants, an oiled wool sweater, his smelly peacoat, a cap and the boots that he wore. Mrs. Pease handed him two notebooks and told him that he had to keep a journal of his voyage to show to his family when he arrived in Kobe. She told him to write the date in the upper corner of each page and tell the story of the day. "I don't know how you write all of this in Japanese, but you must make a record of your trip. I know your Aunt and Uncle will be interested," she said. "In this other book, I want you to draw pictures of what you see on this voyage and send the notebook back to Joe with Captain Sweetser. This will be our secret, Tashi. I know Joe will treasure your pictures."

She put the two notebooks and two pencils in his bag. Tashi thanked her.

Sailing home to Japan on this new bark, the *Astral,* had been arranged by Captain Pease. Tashi would work for his passage. He would assist the old steward, Brian Nichols. Nichols, too old to sail, wanted to go "out east" one more time and he wanted to sail on this new steel hulled bark being launched in the river before their eyes. Tashi would bunk with Nichols and help with his duties of serving and caring for the Sweetser family. Tashi would also help Sung Lee, the Chinese cook, in the galley. In addition to his crew duties, Tashi had been assigned to teach Mrs. Sweetser and the girls how to do Japanese *sumi-e* painting. Tashi's Aunt Lei had taught him this traditional Japanese brush stroke painting. The brush strokes were fluid and looked simple but were hard to master. Hard work would be the ticket for his passage home. Tashi was willing.

"Look, Tashi, the tug is pushing the *Astral*," said Billy.

Sure enough a red tugboat shoved the huge bark out into the river. They watched as the little boat maneuvered the bark to a berth where sailors took the heavy hawsers from the deck and made them fast to the bollards on the wharf. At this point the gangplank was set in place, and the crowd from the platform descended to the wharf and started to board the ship. The townspeople formed a line behind them, so that they, too, could see the new vessel that they had watched being built for almost a whole year.

"Okay, boys, we're going ashore. Lower the dinghy." Captain Pease directed the boys as they lowered the rowboat hanging from the davits on the stern of the *French*. The little green rowboat was named *Pease Pod.* Tashi picked up his duffle bag and started to heave it into the dinghy.

"Leave it on the *French*, Tashi, we'll spend your last night here, together," said Captain Pease.

Tashi put his duffle bag back in the cabin and the three boys climbed into the little boat. Joe picked up the oars and rowed them to the wharf, where they climbed ashore and joined the line of people waiting to board the Astral for a grand tour.

Once on deck, Tashi felt right at home. The *Astral* had four huge masts just like the *Sindia*. The three forward masts were rigged with the huge yards that would hold the big square sails. The aft mast was rigged like the schooner, *French*. Tashi walked with the Pease family all over the deck and they finally came to the cookhouse.

"This is where I peel potatoes," said Tashi with a grin, "and scrub pots. I will work hard."

"Except for when you are painting with Clarabel and Susie," giggled Joe.

"Don't worry Tashi, Joe is just joshing you. Many brave captains have artistic talents. Captain Nichols does embroidery; my friend Captain Peabody makes crocheted tablecloths, lots of captains paint ship portraits. Joe is just jealous that you get to go on this blue water trip half way round the world." Captain Pease laughed. "But I must tell you, it is a bit unusual for the cabin boy to be giving painting lessons to the captain's wife and daughters. Never mind, whatever it takes to get you home."

Next they entered the captain's quarters where the whole Sweetser family was busily shaking hands with the visitors and accepting congratulations and best wishes. Their saloon looked like a miniature living room complete with built in sofas and a small piano bolted to the deck. On the floor were Persian carpets and there were pictures of Maine bolted to the bulkheads. Mrs. Sweetser was not going to do without her comforts on this trip. Overhead, the skylight let in the late afternoon sun, giving a warm glow to the crowded cabin.

"Hello, Joe," said Clarabel. "Tashi, I am glad you are coming with us."

"Captain Pease," Captain Sweetser bellowed in his large voice, "come and see my new collection of charts. Tomorrow we load our first round of provisions and the next day the steamer will arrive to tow us to New York. Wish I could sail, but our sails are waiting to be put on in New York. It will take us only two days to get to the city, if we are lucky. We have one last night ashore."

"I'll see you at dawn, young man." He directed those words to Tashi.

"Aye, sir," replied Tashi.

"Tashi will be on board when the sun rises," said Captain Pease.

"That will be fine. Mr. Nichols, come here," beckoned Captain Sweetser to the old bent man who was following the visitors around the cabin, making sure they did not touch any of Mrs. Sweetser's pretties.

"Captain," he replied.

"This young lad, Tashi, will be your helper for the voyage. We are taking him home to Japan. Captain Pease tells me he is a good worker. Show him his bunk."

The boys and Captain Pease followed the stooped over grumbling man. He was very disagreeable; he smelled sour and looked it, too. Joe and Billy made faces at Tashi, letting him know they could hear what Nichols had to say.

"What am I to do with this slanty-eyed boy in my cabin? I hope he is quiet and does his work. What must the captain be thinking? This is not a passenger ship," he muttered, as they crossed the companionway into a small cabin with bunk beds on one wall. "Yours is the top bunk and I'll have no beds unmade in my cabin," Nichols grumbled some more.

Tashi bowed to Mr. Nichols and said, "Thank you. I will work hard."

By the time they got up on deck it was empty and getting cold. For a brisk January evening there was no wind and the harbor was like a mirror reflecting the sun setting over the Maine hills.

"Look at those masts," said Joe. "Tashi, have you ever gone aloft?"

"Once, on the *Sindia*. It is very beautiful up top with the birds. I only climbed as far as the crow's nest, never out on the yards," he admitted.

"Wish I could go aloft," said Joe.

"What's stopping you?" said the booming voice of Captain Sweetser. "What say you, Captain Pease? Can the boys go up? Never to soon to get their sea legs, I say."

"They can, if I can go with them." Captain Pease replied.

"Be my guests, and I wish my old knees would allow me to come along," replied Captain Sweetser.

"Boys have all the fun!" chimed in Clarabel, who stood there watching the proceedings. It was evident that she would have climbed right up the ratlines with the boys, but she was wearing a long skirt and her mother would have never allowed her to do such a thing.

Tashi went first up the starboard ratlines, Joe right behind him, then Billy, and last of all Captain Pease. They climbed the mainmast up to the yards of the topgallants where the crow's nest jutted out to from a small platform. All four bodies crowded into the crow's nest.

"This is as far as we go boys. We're not going out the yards. Look around. I hope you know how hard this rigging is to climb when the wind is blowing hard and the rain is cutting into your face like little needles. Tonight is a beautiful calm night and we're standing in the perfect place to watch the sun go down. The sky is raging red, Tashi, a good omen for your trip tomorrow. Down we go, boys. And you are not to tell your mother we did this," Captain Pease led the way down the ratlines.

"How far could you see?" queried Clarabel. "It's not fair that girls can't go aloft."

"You go," said Susie, "I am staying on deck and I'd rather stay ashore with Granny."

Clarabel looked at her sister. "You are such a scaredy cat."

Tashi and Joe and Billy, all three, told Clarabel that they could see the top of the hills and the light down the river. Best of all the sunset blazed red over everything. Now darkness fell, and it was time to return to the *French*.

Once aboard their schooner, Captain Pease made Tashi's impending departure more certain by saying, "Okay, boys, Let's take a look at the map and see where Tashi is going. Don't have a real chart. All I have is this old world map aboard to remind me of how big the oceans are. It will serve the purpose."

"Clarabel showed our whole class where they would be sailing. She thinks she is so smart," muttered Joe.

"Well, let's see if she was correct and show Billy where Tashi is going." Captain Pease spread the crackling old map on the table.

"Here we are in Maine. Here is New York. Tashi will sail across the Atlantic Ocean and go round the tip of Africa at the Cape of Good Hope."

"Is the Cape of Good Hope as dangerous as Cape Horn?" asked Tashi.

"Can be but doesn't have to be," answered Captain Pease. "The rough spot is right here," and he pointed to an area a little south of Africa. "This place is called the 'roaring forties' where the wind can blow like blazes. You may sail around with no trouble at all. Let's hope for a smooth passage. Once around the Cape you will sail to Christmas Island, which is near the entrance to the Straits of Sunda. Then you will wiggle through this passage into the China Sea. Once in Shanghai, you can find passage to Japan, or perhaps by then Captain Sweetser will have a manifest to pick up cargo in Kobe. Japan is far away, Tashi. I am honored to have had you as my guest for this brief time." Captain Pease shook Tashi's hand.

"I was lucky to find you. Thank you for helping me go home," Tashi bowed to Captain Pease and joined the boys in the bunks.

"Tashi, when you cross the equator just throw this overboard and let's see if the currents bring it back to Maine. I've put my name and address inside so the bottle will be returned to me wherever it makes landfall. I'm going to miss you."

Joe placed a small bottle in Tashi's hand, and crawled under the covers.

"Good night, Tashi," whispered Billy.

Chapter 9

Return to New York Harbor

IN THE MISTY HAZE OF MORNING, Tashi, stood on the deck of the *Astral,* and watched the *French* sail away. This could be the last time he would ever see his pal, Joe, and the Pease family. As happy as he was to be headed home, it was a sad moment for Tashi. In his pocket he fingered the small bottle that Joe had given him last night tightly corked and sealed.

He watched till he could no longer see the schooner. All the while, box after box, and huge burlap bags were carted aboard the *Astral.* Some of the cargo carried up the gangplank was deposited in the galley. Some things were stowed in the hold. Then, Tashi heard a commotion coming from the wharf. He ran to the side of the vessel to see what was happening. Mrs. Sweetser and Clarabel were climbing the gangplank but Susie stood on the dock wailing.

"I won't go! I won't go aboard without Tommy." Clutched in her arms was a big straggly tiger cat. The cat cried with Susie and had his claws fastened to her shoulder holding on. Captain Sweeter's bald head shone bright red. He tugged on Susie's arm but she did not move. Clarabel kept looking back over her shoulder scornfully. When aboard, she ran right over to Tashi.

"Morning, Tashi, Susie found that old stray cat last night and he followed us home to Granny's house. She convinced Granny to give him some milk. Well, he was still on the porch this morning and he followed us to the wharf. Susie says she is not coming without him. Papa says the cat has too many fleas to come aboard. I think the cat will come with us or Susie will keep on crying. Papa can't stand it when Susie cries. I never cry."

Tashi smiled seeing this tiny girl getting her way with the captain of a huge sailing ship.

Pretty soon Captain Sweetser walked up the gangplank leaving Susie standing on the wharf holding the cat. When he reached the deck he ordered one of the sailors, "Go down and get them. Just haul them aboard."

By this time, Susie attempted to walk up the steep gangplank holding the howling cat. She stumbled as she cried and clutched the cat and tried to hold the rail. The brawny sailor simply picked up the child and the cat and carried them up the steep gangplank. Once aboard, the cat ran away from Susie, which brought on more cries.

"Susie, that is enough. The cat is on board. The steamer is waiting. We are going to New York." Mrs. Sweetser was annoyed with her young daughter. "Into your cabin and help Clarabel arrange your things."

Tashi watched the mother and the girls head to their cabin. Susie was still crying. Clarabel hung behind and ran over to Tashi and said, "Please come and get me when we cast off the lines. I want to be on deck when we leave Bath."

Tashi nodded. After the cargo was loaded and the crew aboard, all hands came up on deck as the *Astral* was to be towed to New York to get her sails and manifest for the voyage to the far east. Tashi went to the captain's quarters and called Clarabel to come on deck. She joined him at the rail of the quarterdeck to watch the sailors work together to attach the *Astral* to the tow steamship.

Standard Oil's steamship, *Maverick*, towline attached, pulled *Astral* from its berth. In two days they would be in New York harbor. She eased away from the pier and headed down river.

"Good bye to Maine," Clarabel mused. "I am so happy to be going to sea. I am the only girl in my class at school who will have seen China and Japan. It is so exciting. Isn't it Tashi?"

Tashi smiled. He was glad to be going home.

It was a strange sight to see a huge sailing vessel being towed down river by a steamship. On their journey down the coast they would pass Gay Head Light on Martha's Vineyard, to starboard; they would then look for the light at Montauk Point at the northern end of Long Island. The Fire Island Light, known as the "winking lady" would be next. Finally, when they saw the Coney Island Light at Norton's Point, they would turn to enter the main channel to New York Harbor. The captain on the *Maverick* knew these waters as though they were his own back yard, and steered his little boat, towing the giant four-masted bark as easily as a farmer might tow a hay cart.

The sails for the *Astral* were being made in New York. After a brief stop to pick up her sails, the *Astral* would again be towed to Bayonne, New Jersey, to load the cargo of case oil for delivery to Shanghai. Sailing ships traveled faster than any other vessels on the open seas. In port, the giant sailing ships could not maneuver in close quarters, thus needing the help of towboats and tugs to get around the harbor.

Mrs. Sweetser kept the steward busy arranging their cabin and all of their possessions. She stowed away all of the clothes and made sure the cook understood what the family would like to eat for dinner. The two days passed quickly because of all of the work that needed to be done. Tashi helped the cook in the kitchen and also helped the steward, who grumbled constantly and never told Tashi what to do, he just yelled at him. The poor boy was well aware that he was not welcome to share Nichols' cabin.

"Keep out of my things," Nichols snapped at Tashi. "I don't like having you in my cabin and I don't want you in my things." He assigned Tashi one little cubby hole and took over the rest of the cabin. "You stay away from those little girls. I don't think you should even talk to those girls. Just stay away!"

Just then came a knock at their door. A sailor stuck his head in the cabin and said, "The captain's lady wants Tashi in their cabin, pronto!"

Tashi jumped from his bunk and headed out the door. Nichols muttering in the background, "This ain't right, it just ain't right. I am their steward."

The captain's quarters had been stripped bare for the journey. Rugs rolled and stowed away, cushions off the furniture, all of the chairs and tables fastened to the deck so they wouldn't slide around. Standing in the center of the saloon was a big table on which they ate their meals, played their games, and wrote letters. It was the center of activity. A cabin for the girls opened off this big room, as did another cabin shared by the captain and his wife. Mrs. Sweetser asked Tashi to come into the saloon.

"Tashi, I want to start our painting lessons. Can we start now?"

On the table were paper, brushes, ink sticks and all of the other things needed to paint.

Tashi quickly organized the tools in the fashion required. Brush on the right, water glass at the top, ink stick and pan in the proper place.

Clarabel, Susie and their mother watched him get set to paint.

"Today we paint bamboo and leaves. You must practice again and again." Tashi said. He dipped the ink stick in the water and rubbed it in the little dish. Then he filled his brush with ink and tested it on a spare piece of paper. Quietly he painted, using his brush to form stems and leaves. In only a few swishes and strokes, he had painted his picture.

"Now, you do."

The three picked up their brushes and began to paint. Tashi quietly left them to work.

On the day before, under Mrs. Sweetser's direction, he had helped organize the family quarters. Tashi marveled at the amount of luggage brought aboard for Mrs. Sweetser and the two girls. He could not begin to imagine what was in all of those steamer trunks. He now knew that there was enough paint and paper for all of them to learn to paint in the Japanese manner of sumi-e. One step at a time, Tashi began the lessons.

Entering New York Harbor, they passed the Statue of Liberty to port, with the Sweetser family all on deck to give her their greeting. Maverick towed them to South Street wharf. As they neared the Brooklyn Bridge, all hands stopped their work for a minute to see the spectacular bridge. These men from Maine were proud of this bridge, built of Maine granite coasted to New York on schooners just like the *Lewis R. French.* They cheered as they sighted the bridge.

The steamship dropped its towline and the tugboat, *Admiral Dewey,* pushed the big bark into the wharf on Front Street in New York. The sailors tied the vessel in its berth and settled in for dinner aboard.

Tashi assisted Nichols serving the dinner.

"You just do as I tell you and don't say a word," Nichols grumbled at Tashi.

They carried platters from the galley to the sideboard near the table. Tashi ran back and forth to the galley with the hot food. Nichols set the table and showed Tashi where the silver and glasses were to be placed.

"The family and the first officer will sit here," he said. "I will put the food on the table and they will serve themselves. You can pour the water and fix the tea and coffee. I don't want you to say one word. Do you understand?"

Tashi nodded. He understood.

"After they have eaten you will carry all the dishes to the galley and help Sung Lee wash up. That's your job." Nichols gave the boy a nasty look and Tashi continued his back and forth with all the food.

The captain and his family came into the dining room. The captain sat at one end of the table, Mrs. Sweetser at the other end, Clarabel and Susie on one side. There were two chairs on the other side, but only one was used by the first officer.

"Nichols, What's for dinner? I'm hungry," said Captain Sweetser.

"Roast beef tonight, sir", said Nichols as he placed the food on the table. Tashi was right behind him handing him platters and serving utensils.

"Tashi, we loved our painting class, and each of us has practiced bamboo painting. Susie wants to paint a cat. Can we do that tomorrow?" Mrs. Sweetser asked Tashi, who stopped what he was doing, looked at her, then looked at Nichols, and wondered what he was supposed to do. He just stood still.

"Cat got your tongue, boy?" the captain boomed. "Answer the lady."

"Too soon to paint cats. Must learn to do some other things first, " Tashi answered as Nichols glared at him.

Susie and Clarabel both asked Tashi questions, which he answered as Nichols, stamped around the room. Tashi knew that Nichols thought it wasn't right that the girls spoke directly to Tashi and wanted him to answer. Tashi also knew that he had to be polite to the girls and respectful to Nichols. He was accustomed to being respectful to elders, even grumpy, nasty elders like Nichols.

When dinner was over and Tashi had carried all of the dishes into the galley, Nichols sat on a chair while Tashi washed the dishes.

"You should not be talking to the captain's family. It just ain't right," he muttered. Nichols was very unhappy about the whole situation. Tashi just washed the dishes and was very quiet. He understood that Nichols did not understand his relationship with the captain and his family. For that matter, Tashi wasn't sure that he understood. He knew that it was important for him to be polite to everyone. He bowed to Nichols to let him know he'd heard his words and finished the dishes.

Morning brought much activity. Sail makers boarded the *Astral* and cart after cart delivered the huge sails to the pier where they were carried aboard the ship. Sixteen huge canvas sails were attached to the wide yards on the three forward masts. More than forty men, sailors and riggers, were aloft in the rigging bending on the sails. The spanker was run up the aft mast to be sure of its cut. All day, the sailors and the riggers worked together to be sure the sails were just right. All of the jibs and staysails were stowed in their proper lockers.

After the morning meal, Tashi found a safe place on deck to watch the action. He crouched on the quarterdeck out of the way, amazed at the difficult task being accomplished overhead. These huge sails would power this ship to take them around the world.

"I've never watched them put on the new sails," said a voice. There was Clarabel standing behind him. "It's really hard to haul those sails up that high. Those sailors must be very strong. You could never do that, Tashi."

Tashi listened to the girl prattle, wondering if she ever tired of talking.

"Good thing the wind isn't blowing today or we'd be sailing right into those buildings," Clarabel said to Tashi and pointed to the row of red brick buildings on Front Street across from their wharf.

"There is lots of wind in the Atlantic," replied Tashi, "no need for wind now."

The two continued to watch the activity. Susie and her mother remained in the cabin trying hard to make it look like any other living room ashore. All of their work would be packed up and stowed away when the ship sailed. Because the vessel rolled and tossed in the waves of the ocean, there could be no rugs on the decks or fancy vases filled with flowers on the tabletops. Even the largest ships were seldom flat on the sea. Sailing vessels leaned and rocked and moved with the motion of the ocean and the wind. At this moment, in the cold clear day in New York Harbor, everyone aboard the Astral was thankful for no wind.

"Clarabel, come here please. You must get ready. We are going to the opera." Mrs. Sweetser called to her daughter.

"Mother, I am watching them bend on the sails," replied Clarabel.

"Those men do not need you to help them do their work. Come here, you must be dressed for the opera."

"I *am* dressed," replied Clarabel.

"You are not going to the Metropolitan Opera dressed in that old coat and dress, young lady. Come here!"

Clarabel left Tashi and went below. Tashi changed his perch and went forward. He crawled out on the bowsprit and stretched out in the net that was rigged under it. From that position, looking up, he could see all of the men in the yards rigging the sails. Captain Sweetser stood on the deck watching every action.

At dusk, the sailors and sail makers descended from the high rigging. The sail rigging crew departed for their homes and families, while the Astral's sailors headed to the galley for their evening meal.

At seven o'clock, the captain, Mrs. Sweetser and the two girls appeared on deck. A hansom cab drawn by a dapple-gray horse waited at the bottom of the gangplank. Tashi watched the family descend the gangplank and get into the waiting cab. The girls wore dark blue velvet capes with fur-trimmed hoods. Mrs. Sweetser was elegantly enveloped in black velvet. Captain Sweetser looked dapper in his jacket dotted with brass buttons. The first mate lowered the gangplank for them and raised the gangplank when the captain and his family had stepped ashore. The crew was not permitted to go ashore, for fear they would not return. Tomorrow at dawn, the *Astral* would be taken to Bayonne to load on the case oil. The gangplank would be lowered for the captain and his family when they returned later that evening.

"Why would anyone want to go hear a screeching opera," grumbled Nichols. "I'm going to have to fix them a midnight meal when they come in. What do they think I am, their maid?"

Nichols went to bed early, grumbling about the captain and his family expecting a meal when they returned late at night.

"I will stay up and wait for the family," Tashi had told the disagreeable old man. Tashi was glad to be rid of Nichols for a while.

While he waited in the warm galley, Tashi fixed himself a cup of tea. The galley smelled of stale coffee and sweaty sailors. Tashi finished his tea and got out his notebook that Mrs. Pease had given him. He wrote about the ship being towed to New York from Maine. He described little Susie and her straggly cat and Clarabel asking a million questions when the huge sails were being bent on the yards. He wrote about how sad it was to leave the Pease family and how he wished his family in Japan could know them. Tashi knew it was unlikely he would ever go to Maine again. He laid his head on his arms on the table and fell asleep.

Screech! Rumble! Tashi heard the gangplank being lowered into place for the Sweetsers to come aboard. He went topside to greet them.

Clarabel was first up the gangplank. With her cape flowing behind her, she jumped onto the deck. "It was so romantic, Tashi, we saw the opera, *Der Fliegende Hollander.* That's German for "The Flying Dutchman". It was all about the Dutch captain who was doomed to sail the seas for eternity and Senta, the girl who loved him. The music was beautiful and so was Senta. Their love was doomed, yet she proved her love by following him. Some say the ship was sunk, but I think it is still sailing. I guess it would be called a ghost ship. I do hope to see the Dutchman sailing in the moonlight." Clarabel danced around the deck, her blue cape floating as she twirled.

"You'd better hope to not see the Dutchman young lady," said Mrs. Sweetser, "If you see that ship, the legend says that we might never see land again."

All of this talk about ghost ships confused Tashi. He asked the Sweetsers if they would like to have something to eat or drink.

"Oh yes, Tashi, let's have some tea and some of that lemon cake we did not have time to eat earlier," replied Mrs. Sweetser.

Tashi headed for the galley to make a pot of chamomile tea. He put slices of cake on a plate loaded a tray and carried it back to the captain's quarters. The family ate their cake and drank their tea. Tashi waited in the companionway for them to finish. He was tired. At last Mrs. Sweetser called for him to take the tray back to the galley.

Tashi cleared the dishes onto a big tray. Clarabel stopped him as he headed to the galley.

"Look Tashi! This is my program from the opera," Clarabel showed Tashi a book with photos of people singing on a fancy stage. "I just loved the opera. I do wish you could have seen it too. Maybe Japanese boys don't like opera," she mused.

Tashi wondered what she meant by that. Japanese boys liked to hear singing and loved to go to the theatre. He and Sami had gone to the theatre with his Aunt and Uncle. Clarabel was a silly girl. He did not understand her ways and was sure she did not understand his. Girls as dramatic and unruly as Clarabel would be made to be quiet and calm in Japan. Here, Clarabel danced on the deck and sang with her mother and father smiling and he, a stranger, watching. In Japan, girls could be silly behind closed doors but not in front of strangers.

He returned the tray to the galley, washed the cups and plates and put them away. His work finished, he went to his cabin. Nichols' snoring roared through the door. Tashi couldn't help but chuckle at the raucous noise he'd managed to learn to sleep with. He crawled under his covers and thought about his brother Sami in Japan and Clarabel dancing on the deck singing her opera.

Chapter 10

Stowaways

TOOT, TOOT! THE TUGBOAT, *Helen McAllister,* signaled the *Astral.* The tug was in place to take the *Astral* down river to load her cargo. With much shoving and maneuvering the *Helen McAllister* got the huge vessel out of dock and into the East River. The small tugboat pushed the *Astral* to the loading dock at Constable Hook in Bayonne, New Jersey.

Mrs. Sweetser and Susie decided that they did not like to be out on deck in the cold blustery winds of January. Clarabel, however, seldom went below except to eat. She wore on her head a navy blue knitted watch cap, just like the other sailors. Her long red curls sprung from under it and blew into her eyes, yet kept her neck warm. She wore mittens, and had convinced her father to give her a warm wool pea coat from the Slop Chest, the ship's store where the sailors bought their gear, should they need something. Clarabel would have worn the warm trousers that were in the store for the sailors, but her mother would not approve. She wore her woolen skirt with the jacket and hat. Even this unusual attire distressed her mother, but her father was glad to have his daughter on deck with him.

"Look, there is the Statue of Liberty!" Clarabel exclaimed." She is the queen of the harbor. I am so happy to see her."

Tashi, in position with his notebook quickly sketched the lady as they sailed by.

"Let me see, Tashi, what are you drawing?" Clarabel asked.

Tashi showed her a picture of the tug in front of the Statue of Liberty. The notebook, his gift from Mrs. Pease, was precious to him. Tashi drew what he saw. The *Astral* passed the Statue of Liberty with the tug between it and the statue.

"Tashi that is exactly how she looks. Do you think I can learn to draw like that?" Clarabel stood at his shoulder watching him sketch.

"Father, look at this," she summoned the captain to see Tashi's drawing.

"Boy, you are good at that."

"Where did you get that notebook, Tashi?" she asked.

"Mrs. Pease gave it to me. She asked that I draw pictures for Joe and ask someone to bring the notebook back to Maine for him. I will do that," replied Tashi.

Without asking, Clarabel took the notebook and pencil from Tashi and began to write on the next page. When she finished she handed the notebook back to him. "Joe can't read your funny Japanese letters so I will write about your pictures. That way he'll know what you're drawing. Just bring the pictures to me and I'll write about them. That's what we should do."

"Yes, Miss Clarabel," replied Tashi.

"I am not Miss Clarabel, I'm just Clarabel, Tashi. Sometimes you are so dumb."

She walked away leaving Tashi wondering what he had done to annoy her.

It took two weeks to load the 133,000 cases of oil aboard. During that time, the crew from Maine would continue to organize and get ready for its crossing. At some point nearer to departure, the first mate arrived and with him ten more sailors making the total crew: twenty~eight sailors, a cook, first and second mates, Nichols, Tashi, Captain Sweetser, his wife and Clarabel and Susie. Mrs. Sweetser and the girls never ventured forward of the quarterdeck on the aft section of the deck. That way they had contact only with the helmsman, the steward, the cook, the two mates and Tashi. Their world and that of the sailors seldom coincided.

Tashi wandered back and forth between his berth with the steward and the crew in the foc'sle. He drew pictures of the crew and the vessel from all angles. Later on under sail, Tashi's time would be taken up with deck work, but, at the moment, he only helped with the meals for the captain's family and drew pictures.

The kerosene loaded aboard was packaged in large square tin cans, which were then contained by a wooden case just light enough for a man to carry. On February 8, 1902, the tugboat, *Helen McAllister,* arrived with a pilot who boarded the *Astral*. With much fanfare and tooting the big bark was towed to Sandy Hook Light where the pilot disembarked. All hands were on deck to watch the tug depart. Able-bodied seamen scurried about in the rigging preparing to set the sails. Tashi and the girls watched from the quarterdeck as the new, white sails were unfurled from the yards. A fresh breeze filled the sails and the *Astral* slowly began to sail under her own power. Within the hour all sails were set and the *Astral* was making good speed. Her bow cut through the waves like a giant steel knife. The

Astral was on her way to the Far East and Tashi was on his way home.

The rhythm of working on a big sailing ship began. The crew was divided into two groups, port watch and starboard watch, each group was on watch for four hours at a time round the clock. The call for "all hands on deck" which required everyone to help, could come at any time. The *Astral* sailed with everyone working. Tashi did not stand watch but was on call whenever the cook or the steward or Captain Sweetser and his family needed him.

"Tommy, Tommy," called Susie. It was the first time in days that Susie had come out on deck.

"Where is my kitty?" she asked John Loeper, first mate, and officer on duty. Tashi coming out of the cookhouse heard her calling the cat and heard the mate reply.

"I haven't seen the kitty today, Miss Susie."

"Please help me find him," said Susie to the mate. "I am afraid that he will wash over board."

"Don't you worry about that, Miss, that cat is not leaving this ship. It's his meal ticket."

The officer smiled at the little girl.

Susie walked around the quarter deck calling, "Here, kitty, kitty. Here, Tommy, where are you?" The sailors on duty smiled as they watched the child looking desperately for her cat.

Tashi wondered where Tommy could be. Usually the cat lounged by the stove in the galley, or in the main cabin, curled up on one of the divans, much to the chagrin of Captain Sweetser. After lunch, Tashi would take a look around and see if he could find Tommy.

Tashi served dinner to the family. The girls were not happy to see split pea soup again, but they ate all of the baked ham and scalloped potatoes. Susie complained that she did not want to eat until she found her kitten.

"Susie, settle down and eat your dinner. Eat the last of the apples. Remember what they taste like as you will not see another for a long time, and don't worry about that cat, "Mrs. Sweetser admonished her daughter.

Late in the afternoon, the sky was overcast and dark clouds formed on the horizon. All sails bellied full and the vessel moved along at great speed. Tashi listened to the wind whistling through the rigging and heard the slap, slap of the bow as she cut through the dark blue water. He wandered around the deck looking for the cat. Passing the starboard sail locker, he heard a squeaking noise. He opened the hatch on the locker and there was Tommy with three little kittens suckling on her.

Tashi smiled and stroked the kitty. He then returned to the captain's quarters and knocked on the door to the saloon.

"Who is it?" asked Mrs. Sweetser.

"It's Tashi," he answered.

Tashi entered and said, "I found Tommy. Come with me."

He led Susie and Clarabel and Mrs. Sweetser out on deck and started toward the bow on the starboard side.

"Girls, I don't want you to go down there," said the captain .

"Captain, I found the cat and want to show Susie and Clarabel. Please come with us," said Tashi quietly to the captain .

Judging the determined look on Susie's face, and listening to the girls clamor that they had to go with Tashi, the captain decided to accompany Tashi and his family forward on the ship. Tashi opened the hatch on the sail locker to reveal Tommy and her kittens.

"Well, can you believe it? Tommy is a mother," said Captain Sweetser.

"They are so cute," said Susie, reaching for a kitten.

"Don't touch them," said Mrs. Sweetser. "Mother cats don't like to have their kittens touched until they are a little bigger than this, Susie. Be careful. We will have Tashi move Tommy and her kittens to the stateroom so you can keep an eye on them and she won't have so far to go for food. Tashi, go find a basket for these kittens." Mrs. Sweetser knew just what to do for the new mewling kittens.

Tashi found a basket in the storeroom off the galley and took it forward. Carefully he picked up Tommy and her kittens and took them aft to the captain's quarters. For the rest of the evening he and the girls watched the kittens and fed Tommy.

"Are you going to give Tommy a new name, Susie?" asked Clarabel.

"No, Tommy is Tommy, and who cares if he is a she? I love these kitties," replied Susie.

Days went by and Tashi continued to keep track of their progress on the chart laid out in the charthouse. Tashi could see on the chart that they had sailed south from New York, passed Bermuda, and were headed to the southeast off the coast of South America. Captain Sweetser noted Tashi's interest in the charts. He was teaching Clarabel how to take sightings at noon with the sextant. She learned easily, and would chart their course, marking the coordinates on piece of paper by the chart.

"Tashi, come take a look at what we are doing," Captain Sweetser invited the boy to the table.

Tashi watched as Captain Sweetser checked Clarabel's figures. The captain would then copy them or correct them and then mark the chart. More often than not, Clarabel's figures were correct. Tashi listened and learned what she did, but he never wrote on the paper or the chart.

On March 3, Tashi said to Clarabel, "Tomorrow we cross the line."

"You mean the equator," she replied very haughtily. "I don't know why sailors call it 'the line" when it has a perfectly good name.

"Sailors on the *Sindia* all called the equator, the line. I guess it is what you call it after you cross it," he said.

"Tashi, sometimes you just think you are so smart because you have sailed halfway round the world. Well, you don't know everything."

"Have you ever crossed the equator?" Tashi asked.

Clarabel tried hard to show him that she knew more than he did.

"No, and of course neither has Susie," replied Clarabel. "You're just a "know it all" and think you know everything about sailing. Well you don't. I am tired of having you act like you're so smart."

Tashi reached into his pocket and pulled out the bottle that Joe Pease had given him weeks before when they left Maine.

"I am going to throw this bottle in the water today," said Tashi.

"Let me see," said Clarabel taking the bottle from Tashi's hand.

She squinted and could barely read Joe Pease's name scrawled on the paper rolled up in the bottle.

"It's just like Joe Pease to think a bottle can float back to him in Maine from the middle of the Atlantic Ocean. It will never happen," Clarabel was definite when she spoke. "How can you possibly believe that a bottle will find the Maine coast? It's not a homing pigeon, really! Boys can be so simple-minded." Clarabel returned the bottle to Tashi.

"I promised Joe that I would and I will throw it overboard. It might float back to him, Miss Clarabel. Please remember to ask Joe about it when you go back to Maine."

Tashi threw the bottle overboard and they watched it bob in the waves until they could no longer see it.

"I will ask Joe if the bottle washed ashore in Searsport, but I am telling you right now that it won't happen." Clarabel smiled at Tashi, shook her head and walked aft to go below.

Tashi could tell that Clarabel thought that he and Joe were foolish to think this little bottle would float on the sea back to Maine. Tashi knew it was unlikely, but he also knew that they were sailing at the edge of the Gulf Stream which could take the little bottle right back to Maine. Ocean currents were unpredictable and constant at the same time. So, Clarabel didn't know everything.

Tomorrow the *Astral* would cross the equator and Tashi had some preparations to make. Miss Clarabel would remember her first crossing of the equator. Of that, Tashi would make sure.

Chapter 11

Party at Sea

DAWN BROUGHT A ROSY PINK SKY AND A LIGHT WIND blowing from the south. *Astral* had her sails set, but they flopped and fluttered as she tried to maintain her southerly course into the wind. The crew busied themselves cleaning the decks and even painted the inside of the deckhouse as the air was warm and dry on this fair day. Mrs. Sweetser announced it was a good day to do the washing. She ordered some rainwater, saved from the storms the week before, splashed into the large washtub carried on the ship. Tashi and Nichols helped with the laundry and soon the whole quarterdeck was covered with petticoats and sheets and towels draped over every surface. The crew thought it a good idea and joined in the washing. They hung their clothes from the belaying pins round the gunwale forward. The *Astral* was a huge drying rack for wet clothes in the warm tropical sun.

"Ship to starboard," came the cry. The sailor on watch was searching for wind on the water, but instead he spotted a ship sailing slowly toward them in the balmy, southern breeze.

"Ship headed our way," said Captain Sweetser to his wife.

"Oh my," she replied, "just when I turn this ship into a laundry, we get company. Best we take in our clothes. I think they are dry by now."

"Order the laundry to be taken in," said Captain Sweetser to the first mate.

The sailors hurried to take down the laundry and stow it below. They, too, had great pride in the *Astral* did not want to be seen as the laundry ship of the Atlantic. The *Astral* would fly her signal flags from the aft mast and hope to converse with the approaching ship and perhaps send some mail home with her. Clarabel and Susie were in charge of the signal flags. They pulled them out of their box and chose the ones that would signal the other ship to come alongside for mail exchange. First Mate John Loeper directed the girls as to which flags to use. The top flag was always the "S," for Standard Oil, on a bright blue background. The signal flags were run up the aft mast.

Contact with other ships in the middle of the sea was rare but did happen. Social life while in port was expected. Captains' families enjoyed parties, touring and visiting between vessels. Having company aboard would make this unexpected celebration mid-sea a welcome diversion from the long, hot, windless days that had preceded this day.

Mrs. Sweetser started her preparations, hoping the ship was one with a family aboard. If so, she would invite them to come for a visit. Captain Sweetser willingly accommodated his wife's wishes, as this was the very first ship they had seen, and he knew she and the girls would like some company. Mrs. Sweetser ordered the cook to bake a cake. "How far away is the ship?" she asked the captain.

"If this wind holds, she will be alongside in an hour or so. Plenty of time to be ready to entertain," he replied.

Mrs. Sweetser took command. She ordered the deck chairs and a table to be placed on the aft deck. The surrounding sea was as smooth as glass. It was the perfect day for a picnic

"Tashi, tell Sung Lee to be sure to make enough cake for the crew, too. I think we are all in need of a party." Mrs. Sweetser then told the girls to go below and change their clothes. All of this hustle bustle for a party was unusual for a sailing ship. Certainly, it was out of order for the captain's lady to be in charge and giving orders. The aroma of Sung Lee's cake wafted from the cookhouse. The *Astral* was ready for company.

"The ship has veered off to starboard. She's not headed this way," called the sailor on watch, high in the crow's nest.

Clarabel stamped her foot on the deck, "I'm all dressed up for nothing. What a waste of time!" She headed below to change back into her old clothes.

"Not so fast, Missy. We are ready for a party, and a party we shall have. We shall have supper on deck and enjoy this beautiful evening." Mrs. Sweetser could not allow the change in plans to spoil her evening.

Tashi and Nichols hurried to set the table with the good china, and Sung prepared a feast of boiled cabbage and corned beef with custard pudding and sponge cake for dessert. The family enjoyed their dinner without their guests.

The crew changed their watch as Tashi and Nichols cleaned up after the party.

"Who saw that ship?" queried Nichols. "We have enough to do without giving parties for hoity-toity captains and their sniveling brats." He shoved the dishes into a tub and ordered Tashi to take them to the galley.

Nichols just did not know how to enjoy anything.

"Aye, Nichols, I will wash dishes," answered Tashi.

The sky stayed blue and clear but the wind picked up allowing the sails to fill and they continued on their way. Tashi checked the charts and determined that they would cross the equator in the middle of the night. He approached Captain Sweetser.

"Captain, we cross the line in the middle of the night," he said.

"That's true, Tashi, why does that concern you?" Captain Sweetser stared down at the boy.

"King Neptune wants to greet Clarabel and Susie," replied Tashi, grinning at the captain.

"You scalawag," replied the captain, "do you have a plan to initiate the girls as they cross the line?"

"King Neptune would like to serenade the young misses. Do we have your permission, sir?" Tashi asked.

"Put on your finest show. No dunking or splashing the girls. Mrs. Sweetser wouldn't like that." Captain Sweetser chuckled.

Tashi dashed to the foc'sle to engage the crew in this endeavor.

In the dark of night with stars shining on the deck Tashi checked the chart and the time. He determined that the ship had crossed the equator and he gave a signal. All of the sailors on watch began to bang on pots and pans from the galley, and one piped on his flute in a loud, disharmonious din. Captain Sweetser arrived on deck followed by Clarabel and Susie.

"What's all the ruckus?" he asked, and winked at Tashi.

A figure covered in seaweed came forth from the dark. Three sailors illuminated his bearded face with candles.

"We've passed St. Paul's Rock and are in the southern hemisphere. Who here has never crossed the line? Pay homage to King Neptune."

Clarabel and Susie tried to hide behind their father. He took the girls forward and said, "These two have never crossed the line. Bow to King Neptune, girls."

The girls bowed to the figure wearing a crown and brandishing his trident. As quickly as King Neptune appeared, he disappeared, and the sailors began to sing. One of the crew had an accordion which he played as the men sang and danced and performed for the girls in the starlight.

Mrs. Sweetser, wearing her ruffled wrapper, brought each girl a shawl and joined them as they watched the performance. Clarabel and Susie clapped and clapped. Tashi hushed the crowd and pointed to the stars.

"See the cross in the sky," he said pointing to four bright stars. "It is Southern Cross. When you see the cross you have crossed the equator."

"Thank you, Tashi, for making this night very special. God bless our ship and our crew and may this voyage be peaceful," intoned Captain Sweetser, and the sailors all went back to their watch. Tashi remembered the day he crossed the line and the buckets of cold water the crew dumped on him. He shivered at the thought.

Days and days passed as *Astral* sailed across the southern Atlantic. By sailing closer to South America, than Africa they would stay in favorable wind currents. The weather was favoring this voyage, and Clarabel was fast becoming a good, reliable navigator. Captain Sweetser teased her about being an "old salt". If her father was on deck, she was right beside him. For days she kept watch, hoping they would see another ship. As she looked through the spyglass she could see twelve miles across the water in all directions before the curve of the earth would block her view. No ships passed within her range. Even if she spied another vessel, it was doubtful that the *Astral* would alter course to meet it. The delivery of their cargo as fast as possible made money for Standard Oil, Captain Sweetser and the crew.

Clarabel wrote "37 S 12 W" on the paper by the chart. "I am going to look for Tristan da Cunha," she announced, and went on deck. Standing on the deckhouse with the spyglass to her eye, leaning against the mast to steady herself she scanned the horizon. Within minutes, she announced, "There it is, just like the atlas says, a cone-shaped island sticking out of the blue sea."

She handed the glass to Tashi, who had heard her call out the sighting.

"Now we approach the roaring forties," she commented to her friend.

All along, Tashi and Clarabel had worked together on learning to navigate. She would find him and include him in the lesson. He never got to write on the chart, but they worked out the coordinates together before Clarabel jotted them down on paper. He, too, was an accomplished navigator. They were good at taking sights and dead reckoning, which allowed them to know where they were on the vast ocean.

When they went back below, Captain Sweetser looked up from the chart.

"Tashi, I know Captain Pease told you that if we sail through the roaring forties with no trouble, we'll be lucky. Here, take a look a the chart." The captain pointed to the southern ocean, running his finger along the forty degree latitude line. "If this wind holds, we won't have to go that far south."

Tashi looked at the chart and realized there were probably five more weeks of sailing before they got to Christmas Island. He would feel like he was making real progress once they entered the Indian Ocean.

Morning brought dark skies and fierce winds. The motion in the cabin was such that Captain Sweetser put on his oilskins and boots and went up on deck. "Time to shorten sail. Mr. Loeper, have the men secure all gear and be ready for some weather."

"All hands on deck," ordered Officer Loeper.

"Prepare to shorten sail. Furl the mainsails and top gallants," he called.

Some men climbed the ratlines into the high rigging, while others loosened the pin rails and hauled the highest sails on the foremast tight on their yards. Bringing in the upper sails helped the ship cut through the waves without plowing her under. Water was pouring over the decks.

"Ease the halyards. Get those sheets."

Soon the royals, topgallants from the mainmast and mizzen were in their gaskets on the yards. The yards for the courses were lowered so the sails would spill air and not tear. Only the lower topsails remained. These sails maintained stability, as they were smaller than mainsails and higher than the highest waves. As soon as the sails were furled and in the gaskets, the order was given to go stay on course.

Mrs. Sweetser and the girls were in the cabin. They were all in the big bed with the sides pulled up so they would not fall out on the deck. Water sloshed down the companionway and under their door. Susie was crying. Tashi entered the cabin and tried to stuff a rug under the door to keep the water from pouring in and fixed the weather boards. He assured Mrs. Pease and the girls that he would try to keep the water out of their cabin. Clarabel wanted to go out on deck but knew she had to remain below and out of harm's way. Tashi went back to the galley to help Nichols stow away stores and dishes.

The wind raged on. The *Astral* was running with only its spanker and staysails set. *Craaaack!* The noise was heard above the wind and the boom on the spanker splintered and dangled like a broken arm, spilling the force of air from the driving sail. Captain Sweetser maintained his course and held the ship through the storm. As the wind calmed, men cleared the debris, removed the hardware from the broken boom. They would have to rig new one as soon as possible. The *Astral* calmed, with the noise abating, and only the whine of the broken shrouds to remind them of the past weather.

Captain Sweetser went below to check on his family. Tashi and Nichols were bringing in a tray of tea and getting ready to straighten out the disheveled cabin. Tommy and her kittens huddled in bed with Susie and Mrs. Sweetser. Clarabel was picking up papers and books that had fallen on deck and trying to find all of the dominos and return them to their box.

"How are my girls?" boomed Captain Sweetser.

"I hope that is the worst of it," replied his wife. "What was the cracking noise?"

"We lost our spanker boom. Not to worry, we have a spare; it'll be rigged and ready in a couple of days. How did all of this water get into the cabin? Tashi, get a mop."

"We did not have the weather boards on the hatch doors. By the time I realized they were not in place we were wet. Tashi came in and closed them but it was a little late," said Mrs. Sweetser. "I am not much of a sailor and I will surely be glad to see land."

Captain Sweetser comforted his wife and youngest daughter, while Clarabel donned her hat and jacket and went topsides to see what had happened to the ship during the storm. She wanted to find Tashi and hear what he had to say about the storm.

Chapter 12

Wonders at Sea

THE FICKLE WIND THAT DAMAGED THE SHIP changed direction and now helped the ship sail her course. Everyone aboard the *Astral* looked forward to entering the Indian Ocean where the monsoon winds would blow to make their progress easy. The crew worked for two whole days to refit the broken boom. Now all sails were full and by the wind, and the *Astra*l sailed gracefully through the sea.

Tashi continued his painting lessons with Mrs. Sweetser and the girls. Mrs. Sweetser learned everything he taught her and had started to introduce watercolor into her paintings, making them a combination of *sumi-e* and her own style. Tashi was a good teacher and encouraged her to try new ideas. He loved the colors she used with the shades of black and gray ink. Traditional Japanese painting did not have much color. The girls did not have enough patience to be painters. Clarabel especially did not want to sit below in the musty cabin painting when she could be on deck in the wind.

Clarabel had found a place on deck where she could scan the horizon with the spyglass looking for other vessels. She did this for hours at a time.

"What you looking for, Clarabel," asked Tashi of his friend.

"Promise to keep a secret and I will tell you," she replied.

"I promise," whispered Tashi, wondering what she was up to.

"Do you realize where we are?" she asked. "We are sailing around the Cape of Good Hope. You know that. We're close but won't see the coast of Africa. There are better things to see." She stopped and looked at Tashi expecting him to know what she meant.

"What can we see in the open ocean?" Tashi was not following her.

"We can see a ship, a very special ship. You know, the *Flying Dutchman*. This is where she is seen. Right here in the ocean off Good Hope." Clarabel whispered this last bit to Tashi so that there was not a chance of being heard. "I am going to see it, I just know I am."

"Clarabel, that is just a story. The *Flying Dutchman* is not real," Tashi told the girl who was shaking her head as if to say no, no, in real disagreement. She left him standing on the deck and went below to get ready to eat.

After supper, Clarabel asked to be excused from the table and went back out on deck taking up her favorite spot with her spyglass.

"Looking at the stars, Missy?" asked the helmsman as he watched the young girl looking and looking.

"Yes, that's what I'm doing," she replied and looked up rather than scanning the horizon as she had been. It was a clear, bright night and the full moon and the stars made twinkling reflections on the water. The horizon glowed with ambient light from the heavens above. Some luminescent plankton swam in their wake, leaving a trail of sparkles on the water. This night was the sort of night that entrances sailors and makes them go to sea over and over again.

Clarabel suddenly jumped down from her perch on the cabin top. She headed directly to the galley where she knew she would find Tashi washing up the supper dishes.

"Sung Lee, I need Tashi to help me with something," she announced in her most grown up voice.

"Yes, Missy, take the lazy boy with you, he not good at dishwashing," Sung replied.

Tashi, glad to miss out on the dishwashing for one night, followed the girl topside and aft. She looked through the glass and said, "There it is. I can see the ship."

Tashi took the glass and said, "I see nothing." He looked again and scanned the horizon.

She grabbed the glass back from him and pointed it directly aft of the *Astral.* The trail of luminescence following them glowed in the darkness.

"I can see it, look again." She handed the glass back to Tashi.

He did not know what to say. Clarabel was certain, yet he could not see a thing. Tashi was convinced that she was imagining the ghost ship.

"This is our secret, Tashi. You are never to tell a soul that we saw the ghost ship," Clarabel whispered.

"Yes, Clarabel," he replied and handed her the spyglass. He would never tell anyone about something that he could not see.

"Clarabel, where are you?" Mrs. Sweetser called. Clarabel grabbed Tashi's hand and squeezed it before she ran off to answer her mother.

Tashi thought that Clarabel had the most wonderful imagination and knew she would tell fabulous stories when she went home to America. He wished she could tell Sami her incredible tales. Her drama was more exciting than Tashi's quiet story.

Sailing across the Indian Ocean was pure delight. The crew caught flying fish that landed on deck. They cooked the fish and ate a delicious dinner. The monsoons pushed *Astral* north in the warm Indian Ocean. The winds were steady and strong. Lucky for them, there was no rain in these winds, just hot, strong force.

On one particularly beautiful afternoon, Captain Sweetser ordered. "Tashi, get the girls." He was standing by the helmsman looking over the dark blue seas.

"Whale to port," came the call from the seaman on lookout.

"Where are those girls?" Captain Sweetser asked.

Clarabel and Susie came out on deck. Their mother followed them. Tashi carried her folding chair and basket of mending.

"Look, girls, look at that!" Captain Sweetser pointed to two spouts of water in the distance. He told the girls of the whales that lived in these seas, great humpbacked whales that could grow to be fifty feet long and were hunted by whalers. He also told them that they were lucky to see a whale, as the migration did not start for a month or so.

"If we are really lucky we'll see them breach. Now, watch."

The girls watched the spot where they had seen the puff of spray steam up into the air. There was nothing. They kept watching and all of a sudden a big grey form arched out of the water and back in, dragging a huge tail behind.

"Oh, do it again!" squealed Susie. "I want to see it again."

In rapt attention, the girls stood on coiled ropes against the bulkhead so they could peer over the gunwale. At first, nothing happened. All of a sudden the surface of the ocean around them was dotted with dolphins, seemingly flying alongside the *Astral*. As far as you could see there were dolphins jumping out and diving into the water. There were so many that the glorious whales were forgotten. What a sight for two little girls on their first voyage in the Indian Ocean. Tashi watched the excited girls, remembering his first whale sighting in the Pacific Ocean.

As they came closer to Christmas Island and the Straits of Sunda that led to the China Sea, the weather was hot. Sometimes showers would appear out of nowhere, serving to clean the air and the decks of the ship. The crew welcomed the showers and gladly got wet and dried off in the sunshine that came after. Early one morning, a flutter of birds surrounded the ship. Some were familiar gulls and some boobies that the sailors knew and loved, but there were also hundreds of little birds the size of sparrows that nobody onboard could identify. The little birds perched on the rigging and the shrouds, twittered and even dive-bombed some of the sailors.

One little bird hit the deck.

"Captain, we have a passenger," said Tashi as he scooped up the little bird and took him aft to Captain Sweetser.

The captain wrapped his big, beefy hands around the little creature and went off to find his daughters.

"Give it to me," said Susie holding out her hands.

"Be gentle, darling, and let's take it out on deck and hope the little bird will catch its breath and fly away."

The whole group went topside and Susie held the quivering little bird in her hands until it stilled. Then she took it to a coil of rope on deck and set it gently down. It ruffled its feathers, sat and looked at the group of people staring wide-eyed at it and flew off.

"Good bye, little bird," said Susie and waved it away. "I am so glad the little bird came to visit and did not meet up with Tommy." That remark brought on some chuckles as everyone knew that Tommy had been catching birds on deck and eating them, but they had thought that Susie didn't

know about the pussy cat's conquests. Evidently she did.

On May 7, Christmas Island was spotted in the distance. All hands took a look at the little island with the happy knowledge that Java Head was next. Two hundred miles later, and in the middle of the night, the rounded shape of Java Head loomed in the distance. The order was given to slacken all sails and slow the ship to a crawl until daybreak. This passage was narrow. Anjer Roads had been a very busy port before the volcano, Krakatoa, erupted and destroyed the town. Many cargo ships stopped in there to replenish their supplies and have a nice dinner ashore in the English Hotel. Now, they would wait until daybreak to enter this place. Captain Sweetser wanted to see how it looked.

Orders given for sails to be trimmed, the topsails cracked like a gunshot as they filled with air. Making headway to Java Head was exciting. The big green lump in the sea got bigger as they closed in on the shore. Soon they could see the mountains and the fringe of palm trees and golden beaches at the base. As they entered Princess Channel and slid into the Straits of Sunda, there was an air of excitement aboard. When they could see some other vessels in port the captain ordered sails to be shortened to slow progress as they proceeded on their way.

Close enough, they dropped anchor off the coast of Anjer. There was no plan to go ashore. They watched as canoes filled with fresh produce approached the ship. First at the gunwale was Mrs. Sweetser.

"Look at that. Fresh fruit and eggs. I even see a monkey in that boat. Tashi, get Sung Lee out here. We are going to do some shopping." She was thrilled to have some fresh food for their meals. Tashi fetched the cook and they went with her on deck as some of the Malays scrambled deftly up the rope ladders lowered overboard, carrying their wares.

One did bring aboard a monkey, which delighted the girls and caused Susie to exclaim, "Father, I want that monkey!"

"Not a chance, my girl, we have enough crew problems without bringing a monkey aboard."

The little monkey went directly to Susie and sat in her lap and pulled her curls until a sailor was ordered to remove him and send him on his way with the vendors who were clamoring to board the ship and sell their wares.

The shoreline was very beautiful with beaches and palm trees and high, cone shaped mountains surrounding them on all sides.

Nichols told Susie, "Big dragons live on shore and would eat you alive."

"You are teasing me," she replied, "I'm going to tell my father." Nichols laughed and continued stowing away the produce that Mrs. Sweetser was buying as fast as they brought it aboard.

A customs official approached and asked for permission to board. Permission granted, he came aboard and accepted a packet of letters to send back to the United States. He welcomed the *Astral* to Anjer and said how sorry he was that they would not be coming ashore. He told them that the lighthouse had been repaired and there was a very small customs station ashore. However, few Europeans had returned to Anjer. The English

Hotel had not been rebuilt. Those who had returned were glad to see ships and happy to provide them with fresh fruits and vegetables. He would send the package of letters to Batavia to catch the next mail ship.

That night Tashi served the family a feast on deck with fresh eggs and roasted chickens and, for dessert, an array of fruits that were new to Clarabel and Susie. Both girls loved the papayas and mangos and laughed when their mother remarked, "Just think, we will be missing the strawberries in June." How could anyone miss strawberries with these wonderful fruits to eat?

Tashi watched the merriment and, though he enjoyed being with his friends, he wished more than ever to be home with his own family.

Chapter 13

Coordinates: 34.7N 15.2E

DAWN BROUGHT SWIRLING COLORS of pink and orange to the morning sky.

"All hands on deck," came the order from the bridge.

The business of making this huge boat get underway, even with thirty men at their assigned tasks, took some real effort. They weighed anchor and made way.

"Clarabel, Susie, Tashi — look at that." Captain Sweetser pointed to the low rounded island seen in the distance. "About twenty years ago, that was the volcano Krakatoa, that played havoc with this little town. The explosion's force could be felt in Australia. There was a big boom and the red hot lava destroyed the trees and caused a tidal wave that destroyed Anjer. It was a spectacular volcano! Thank goodness it is sleeping today."

Clarabel and Susie looked at the low volcanic island in awe.

"I will be glad to get away from the volcano. Father, where do the dragons live? Nichols told me that dragons lived on shore and that is why we did not go ashore." Susie looked at her father waiting for a reply.

He laughed and explained that there were huge lizards on shore called Komodo dragons. As fierce as they were they did not eat little girls, and it was doubtful that you would see them just going ashore for a visit.

Tashi watched the peaked islands as they passed by and thought of the volcanoes at home in Japan. Japan was a country of volcanic islands just like this. People who lived on those islands were used to seeing volcanoes and enduring coastal storms. He had heard stories about tsunami, huge tidal waves that swamped villages. While it might be exciting to see a volcano erupt, he was glad to be sailing peacefully by this one and getting closer to home.

Tashi had given a letter to one of the tradesmen who had come aboard the ship in Anjer selling fruits. The hope was for the man to give the letter to a sailor on a ship that was bound for Kobe. The letter was addressed to his Uncle in Kobe. It read:

Dear Aunt Lei and Uncle Hiroshi and Sami,

Greetings to each of you. This letter comes from the Straits of Sunda where we have stopped for fresh food. I am the cabin boy on the bark Astral *and we are sailing to Shanghai. Do not worry about me. I am fine. Watch the harbor. I am coming home!*

Your nephew and brother, Takashi

This was Tashi's first chance to send a message home and he did not want to miss it. His family would be waiting for him.

The *Astral* spent a week skirting the shore of Sumatra and sailed through the Gaspar Straits. Lightning storms, short but fierce, plagued them as they journeyed. At last, on June 14 they anchored at Gutzlaff Island, entrance to the Yangtze River and the way to the port of Shanghai.

Tashi looked at the full moon and knew that it was shining over Kobe Harbor. What was his brother Sami doing tonight? Tashi could only hope that his family was well. Closer and closer to home, and almost one year since he sailed away on the *Sindia.*

On the morning of June 16, the *Astral* entered the muddy yellow waters of the Yangtze River. The delta of the river was flat, and the buildings ashore were grey with tile roofs. All along the river sailed traditional Chinese sampans, with their big lateen rigged sails and cargo of families and goods. The river bustled with boat traffic. As they anchored at Wusung, a pilot boarded with a customs official. Plans were made to off-load about twenty thousand cases of oil to lighten the load for the thirty-mile trip up river to Shanghai. Small boats, called lighters, approached the *Astral,* and one by one, the cases of oil were loaded on to the small boats and taken ashore. The rest of the cargo would be off-loaded at a wharf.

With a river pilot on board, and tow steamboat attached, the *Astral* slowly made her way up the final miles on the yellow river to Shanghai, in the midst of sampans and other vessels coming and going, and even the U.S. gun ship, *Wilmington,* which patrolled the river from Shanghai to Hong Kong.

Tashi saw the gun ship and was frightened.

"Is there war?" he asked Captain Sweetser.

"Yes, there is a war in China but it will not get in our way," replied the captain.

Tashi felt very much at home in this hustle bustle of a river. As in Japan, there were families living aboard their boats. He could smell the odors of their fishes cooking in sesame oil, and he knew that many boats from this river called at his Uncle's warehouse in Japan. He was feeling glad to be approaching Shanghai, a familiar name to him and closer still to Japan. Tashi knew that when they left Shanghai, they had only to sail across the China Sea and he would be nearing his home. Captain Sweetser had informed his shipping company that he would like to make a delivery to Kobe or pick up cargo in that port. He hoped to take the boy directly home. Kobe was a busy port on the Inland Sea of Japan. Captain Sweetser had sailed there many times.

The noisy hustle of Shanghai was astounding after the months of quiet lonely sailing at sea. The *Astral* was at anchor, waiting her turn at the loading dock where the case oil would be off loaded.

While the bark was at anchor, the captain hired a sampan to take his family ashore and to visit the other vessels in port. It was the custom to hire a local boat, a sampan, with a local captain to serve as a taxi service while in port. Mrs. Sweetser had her parlor all set up and was ready to entertain. She was also ready to shop in the fine stores along the beautiful

waterfront boulevard in Shanghai. This street, the Bund, was known worldwide for the treasures one could buy there: silk, pearls, spices, and even exotic birds and animals.

Tashi enjoyed his time in Shanghai. He accompanied Mrs. Sweetser and the girls on rounds of shopping and visits to lovely Chinese tea rooms. He carried packages for Mrs. Sweetser and kept the beggars on the street from approaching them.

"Go away," shouted Tashi to the beggars when they came near.

They rode all up and down the avenue by the sea in rickshaws, two wheeled wagons pulled by very strong Chinese men. The men all had long pigtails hanging down their backs. The little girls had not seen this before as their Chinese cook, Sung Lee, had long ago cut his hair and stopped wearing a pigtail.

One morning the signal flags appeared on the bark *Mabel Rickers*, anchored astern of the *Astral.* The message of the fluttering flags asked for a doctor. Captain Sweetser sent the sampan with a sailor aboard to inquire about their problem. The sailor returned with the message, "Captain's wife is about to have a baby."

"I can go help her. I am sure I'd be happy to see another Yankee woman if I were having a baby," declared Mrs. Sweetser, and she took off in the sampan to help with the delivery.

Tashi watched the boat go to the bark at anchor in the distance. He hoped that the baby would be born today, as it was his brother's birthday and had always been a lucky day. Hours later, Mrs. Sweetser returned and announced that a baby boy, named Richard Peabody, was happily delivered, and that she was exhausted.

Everyone aboard the *Astral* was happy with her good news. Captain Sweetser set off some firecrackers in honor of the new arrival. When Captain Peabody saw the fireworks, his crew lighted a display of their own. Tashi and Clarabel watched the display from the top of the aft cabin where Susie would not come. Poor Susie never learned to climb up on the cabin tops or walk on the sloping decks without holding onto something or someone.

The *Astral's* assigned time at the wharf arrived, and for days they were tied alongside while Chinese workers, one after another, carried the rest of the cases of oil off the ship. It took two weeks to off-load their cargo. On July 5, the tug arrived to tow them down the river.

On July 4, all of the American vessels at anchor in the harbor had celebrated their Independence Day by visiting back and forth, from one to another. The hired sampans were busy from morning to night. And most important, Captain Sweetser received an order from his shipping company to pick up cargo in Kobe. He did not know what the cargo would be, but was glad to be sailing to Kobe to take Tashi to his homeport.

Sailing across the East China Sea seemed to take forever. Finally

Tashi saw the shore through the morning haze.

"Tashi, there is Japan! How does it feel, boy, to have sailed around the world?" Captain Sweetser knew the boy was anxious.

"I feel lucky to come home, sir," Tashi replied. All he wanted right now was to be on shore with his brother Sami.

"It won't be long now." Captain Sweetser smiled and watched Tashi and his daughter take the noonday reading with the sextant.

"You mark the chart today, Tashi. We are now in your country and coming to your home," Clarabel handed Tashi the pencil and he wrote the coordinates on the paper by the chart. Even though Clarabel and Tashi seldom made mistakes with their navigating, Captain Sweetser would not allow them to register the course on the charts. That was his job.

Tashi took his bedroll on deck after everyone else was sleeping and slept under the stars. Old Tommy curled at his feet and kept them warm under the covers. The little kittens slept on top of the covers, interrupting his sleep when they chased each other around the deck in the middle of the night. Tashi hoped that Susie would give him one of the kittens when he went ashore in Kobe.

In the morning, as they sailed between the islands on their way to Kobe, Tashi looked at the rocky coastline with its pine trees growing down to the sea. It reminded him of Maine but something was different. He thought about it and laughed. In Maine, the pine tree branches pointed down to the earth. In Japan, the pine tree branches turned up to the sun. Halfway round the world and the trees were the same, yet different. The mountains in Japan were very different from the mountains in Maine, which were rounded and bare and a distance from the sea. Here, in the Inland Sea, in the misty morning, cone-shaped mountains of all sizes erupted from the water. These mountains were painted by every Japanese

brush-stroke painter and made their art, *sumi-e,* loved world wide.

Tashi did not move from his place by the helmsman. Clarabel joined him.

"Oh, Tashi, isn't it beautiful? This looks like the paintings that you and Mother have painted. I can see your inspiration right here. Are you ready?" she asked.

"Ready?" he questioned her. He sometimes wished she would not ask him so many questions.

"You know, ready to see your brother and family, ready to eat fish eyes and rice, ready to go ashore, ready to be rid of me being cranky with you, and my little sister being a pest." She looked at him and smiled.

Tashi laughed, as he knew she was teasing him. It had taken him four months to learn to understand her quirky sense of humor and her sometimes bossy ways. He also realized that he would miss this spunky American girl who had become his friend.

"I'm ready to go home," he answered. Then he handed Clarabel his notebook of pictures. "Clarabel, please take this to Joe."

She accepted the book, leafed through the pages and said, "Tashi, this is beautiful. I am going to look and look at the pictures on our voyage home and memorize all of it. Joe will be so happy to have this. Thank you for trusting me with your book. I will give it to Joe."

"Prepare to lower the anchor," came the order from the bridge.

They would wait for the customs officials and the pilot to come and tell them the procedures to follow for this port. Each city had its own rules and regulations. Cargo ships were at the mercy of customs officials and port pilots. After dinner the pilot arrived. Captain Sweetser got his orders. Tashi handed the pilot a note.

"What was that?" asked Clarabel.

"I sent message to Uncle that I am aboard the *Astral* in Kobe harbor," replied Tashi.

Tashi again slept outside on deck. In the morning he served breakfast to the family, cleaned up the kitchen and returned to his

look-out spot by the wheel. There it was. Flying over the harbor in a long green streak, was a dragon kite.

"May I use the spy glass?" he asked Officer Loeper.

"Sure, Tashi, take a peek," Loeper handed him the glass.

"What are you seeing, Tashi?" asked Clarabel, who had just arrived topside.

"I see my kite, my dragon kite that Sami and Aunt Lei made for me last birthday. It is very long and it is flying in the sky," replied Tashi.

Clarabel took the spyglass. "I see it!" she exclaimed. "I see a beautiful dragon kite with a tail that must be thirty feet long."

She could not see the person flying the kite but she could certainly see the kite. It flew over the ships in harbor and the sampans on the sea. The sun made it glow as it fluttered in the wind.

She handed the glass back to Tashi and saw a tear run down his cheek. He looked again at his kite, and knew his brother Sami was flying it just for him. That kite, meant for all the world to see. "Welcome home, Takashi, Welcome home."

Nautical Glossary

aft ~ toward or at the stern (back end) of a boat or ship.

bark ~ a sailing vessel with three to five masts, all square rigged except the after mast which is fore and aft rigged.

belaying pin ~ a short, removable wooden or metal pin fitted in a hole in the rail of a ship; used for securing running gear.

bend on ~ to fasten a sail to a spar.

bitter end ~ the on board end of a line

bollard ~ a thick post on a ship or wharf used for securing lines or hawsers.

boom ~ pole extending from the mast to hold the foot of the sail.

bow ~ the most forward part of the vessel.

bowsprit ~ a spar, extending forward from the bow.

buoy ~ a float used as a marker.

breach ~ leap of a whale from the sea.

bridge ~ area on a vessel where the wheel is located.

case oil ~ term used for cargo of oil packaged in square cans, four cans to a wooden case, just big enough for one man to be able to load and unload.

cleat ~ a piece of metal with arms used for winding or securing a line.

companionway ~ stair or ladder leading below deck; also a hallway between cabins.

crow's nest ~ a platform high on the mast for a lookout.

davits ~ a small crane that extends over the side of the vessle, used for hoisting.

dead reckoning ~ method of estimating the position of a vessel without using astronomical observations.

Downeaster ~ a sailing vessel built in Maine and sailing from there.

embark ~ to start a voyage.

foc'sle ~ forecastle; a structure at the bow where the crew are housed.

fore ~ toward the bow; prefix indicating this location i.e. foredeck

"full and by" ~ to sail as close a possible to the wind with all sails full.

furl ~ to roll up and secure a sail by tying it to a yard.

galley ~ kitchen on a vessel.

gangplank ~ ramp used to get from the vessel to the pier or wharf.

gaskets ~ canvas strap that secures the square sail to the boom when furled

gunwale ~ upper edge of the side of a vessel.

half model ~ accurate carving of the profile of a ship; can be mounted to a plaque.

halyard ~ line used to hoist sails.

hatch ~ opening in the deck; the cover or door for such an opening.

hawser ~ rope used in mooring or towing a ship or boat.

headstay ~ The wire from the bow or bowsprit to the top of the mast.

helm ~ steering wheel or tiller.

hold ~ space below decks where cargo is stored.

jib ~ a triangular sail attached to the headstay.

lateen rigged ~ sail with a boom at the top and the bottom of the sail.

manifest ~ a list of all the cargo.

main course ~ the lowest square sails.

mast ~ vertical wooden pole on which sails are set.

mizzen ~ a small sail attached to the aft mast.

port ~ the left- hand side of a ship or boat facing forward; often marked with a red light.

quarterdeck ~ aft part of the upper deck of a ship reserved for officers and their families.

ratlines ~ small ropes fastened to the shrouds and forming a ladder for going aloft.

reach ~ any point of sail with the wind coming from the side of the boat

rigging ~ gear used to support and adjust the sails; includes the mast and halyards.

royals ~ the uppermost square sails.

sampan ~ a small Chinese sailing craft.

schooner ~ fore and aft rigged boat with at least two masts, largest sail carried on the aft mast.

sextant ~ navigational instrument used to determine latitude and longitude by measuring the altitude of the sun, moon, and stars.

spanker ~ the after sail of a sailing ship.

spar ~ all poles on a ship that support the mast or the rigging

square sail ~ a sail hung from a yard on the mast.

warp ~ to move a vessel using ropes.

ship ~ a sailing vessel having having three or more square rigged masts.

sound ~ measure the depth of the water.

starboard ~ the right-hand side of a ship or boat facing forward; often marked with a green light

staysail ~ a triangular sail similar to the jib set on a stay forward of the mast and aft of the headstay.

stern ~ back end of a ship or boat

top gallants ~ the square sails above the topsails and below the royals.

topsails ~ the square sails above the main course and below the top gallants.

warp ~ to move a vessel using ropes.

vessel ~ generic term used for large nautical craft.

watch ~ period of time, usually four hours, when part of the ship's crew is on duty.

weather boards ~ boards that slide into hatch openings to keep the water (weather) out of the cabin.

yard ~ a spar or tapered pole hung at right angles to the mast to support the head of a square sail.bio

Mrs. Pease's Molasses Cookies

$^{1}/_{2}$ cup shortening

1 cup sugar

$^{1}/_{2}$ cup water

1 cup molasses

3 $^{1}/_{2}$ cups sifted flour

$^{1}/_{2}$ teaspoon salt

1 teaspoon baking soda

1 $^{1}/_{2}$ teaspoons ground ginger

$^{1}/_{2}$ teaspoon ground clove

$^{1}/_{4}$ teaspoon allspice

sugar to sprinkle on top

Preheat oven to 350 degrees.

Cream together shortening and sugar until light and fluffy. Combine water and molasses. Sift flour with remaining dry ingredients. Alternately add to the shortening mixture the dry and liquid ingredients, blending well after each addition. Chill dough. Roll out to $^{1}/_{8}$" to $^{1}/_{4}$" inch thick; cut with cookie cutter. Sprinkle with sugar and bake on greased cookie sheet for 10-12 minutes.

Makes three dozen 3" cookies.

About the Author

Lucinda Hathaway ("Cinda" to her friends) has traveled all over the world, mostly by ship. She lives, with her husband Jack, in Longboat Key, Florida — a quiet island in the Gulf of Mexico. She had previously lived on another island, Ocean City, New Jersey, and there she became intrigued with the *Sindia*, a steel bark that ran aground in 1901 and became the inspiration for her first book, *Takashi's Voyage*. Her family has vacationed in Maine for almost forty years, so it was natural for her to set this sequel on a Maine Downeaster. She can often be found sailing her sloop *Eventide*. Cinda is happy to share her love of the sea and our natural world with an audience of children eager to learn, and she regularly visits schools to share all of Takashi's stories.

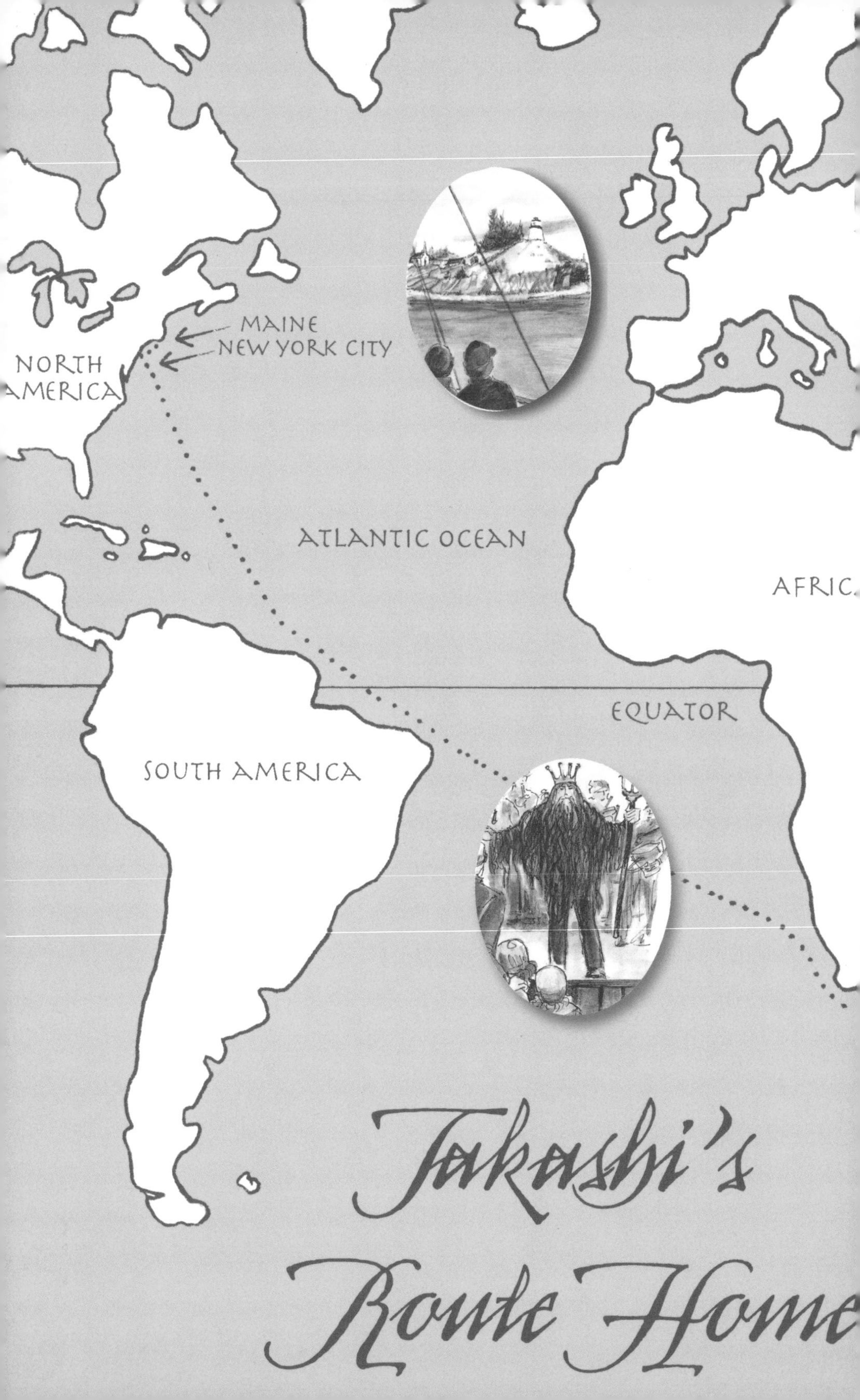
MAINE
NEW YORK CITY
NORTH AMERICA
ATLANTIC OCEAN
AFRIC
EQUATOR
SOUTH AMERICA
Takashi's Route Home